THE TRILOGY OF TIME

SACRIFICE

THE TRILOGY OF TIME

SACRIFICE

SAMANTHA DICKENS

authorHOUSE®

AuthorHouse™
1663 Liberty Drive
Bloomington, IN 47403
www.authorhouse.com
Phone: 1-800-839-8640

Published by AuthorHouse   02/23/2013

ISBN: 978-1-4817-8506-8 (sc)
ISBN: 978-1-4817-8505-1 (hc)
ISBN: 978-1-4817-8507-5 (e)

For my Dad, who never got to see this,
For Bobby, who took me through the journey,
And lastly, for those seeking their true paths.

Chapter 1

The Beginning

"There once was a time when the world was at peace. There was no war, no murder and no violence. This of course was the time before humans arrived upon the earth."

THE EARTH WAS created billions of years ago and on it were placed souls all of equality. These souls each had their own choices to make and feelings to have; and although they were all equal, they were all very different. The creator told these souls that the earth was to be cherished, it was a gift though in itself a curse; of course the nature of the curse was one of the many lessons in which the souls were required to learn to enable them to move on to the next step of their grand journey. For the earth was only to be the beginning for these souls. The creator had given them lessons in which they must learn before they could set foot in his kingdom, utopia. The souls, once their bodies had perished, were reborn upon the earth until all of the creators' lessons were learnt. And so the world began.

Life upon the earth began as a happy existence. The beings that dwelled upon the planet strived upon the lessons in which they were to learn. However they were not told what the lessons were or how many there were in which to learn. So over time the souls were reborn to the earth as their bodies turned frail and died. Some souls learnt quickly and passed on to Utopia having only lived a small number of lives. A number of these souls then greeted the great creator and asked if it were possible to return to the earth to guide others on their paths. The Creator smiled down at these thoughtful souls and chose to bless them with gifts of magic beyond that of the other souls. These were named the elves. They were distinguishable by their slender build, pointed ears, and athletic stamina. They were able to control the earth as no other being could and developed their own language. The elves were of course immortal and therefore never fell ill to any disease, and unlike the other souls of the earth their bodies did not turn weak and frail with age. The other souls failed to accept the elves for what they were and some chose to turn away from them. These were from then on known as humans. The humans did not understand the prospect of a perfect kingdom with the great lord; and what confused them even more was the elves reasoning behind not wanting to stay in Utopia and instead choose to remain upon the earth and aid those who were struggling to perceive the lessons laid down by the Great lord. So over time the humans closed their minds completely, not being able to see further than the ends of their noses. And so it was that their souls were reborn, again and again.

However there were others among the earth's souls that believed the elves. Yet they did not heed the elves advice, or even acknowledge their wisdom. Instead these souls became jealous of the elves; they despised the fact that the elves had seen more, understood more, and in a twisted way, they hated the fact that the elves had beaten them to heaven. So it was then, in the early years of the world that the first battle was fought. These jealous beings chose to attack and rage war upon the land. The elves with their power asked the creator to punish these souls, however he refused. The Great lord was a being that believed in people learning from their own mistakes and left the souls upon the earth to fight among themselves. The elves then took it upon themselves to punish these souls. They banished them to live underground, far away beneath the mountains where they could cause no harm but among themselves. As these angry beings lived in underground tunnels, over time, they became shorter. Their vision adapted to their dark environment and they grew beards that they could tuck in to their belts. They planned in secret to one day over throw the elves and punish the earth for what they thought was betrayal. Though overtime the reason for this feud was forgotten yet the passionate hate remained. And so the dwarves were created. They dwelled on the past and fashioned the world's first weapons. They created axes and short swords, hammers and cross-bows. Yet they never left the safety of their underground home.

Now of course after this great battle the creator was terribly disappointed with the elves. He had trusted them to care for the other beings of the earth, yet instead they had been the cause of a great war. This had angered the great lord enough so that he chose to stop the elves ever returning to Utopia. It was apparent to him that there were still lessons in which the elves were to learn, and he angered at himself at not having seen their lack in understanding before he had granted them passage in to heaven. And so it was that the elves were earth bound. They now despised the Lord for what they thought was treachery and betrayal, and of course complete disregard for all the work in which they had done for the great lord.

The humans now lived alone and over time forgot what should not have been forgotten. The creator saw this and decided to grant them a gift; with this gift he intended to give them a new ray of hope that there was a point to life and that there were still lessons to learn. And so it was that the great creator granted the humans with animals. He hoped that by giving them more souls that they would find what was lost and perhaps move on from the earth. However they did not. Instead of treating animals as equals, in which of course they were, they enslaved them to do their bidding. The humans hunted the creatures and used their dead flesh as large portions of their meals. The great creator was furious and consulted the elves. They refused to help the lord as he had failed to help them in the past. They turned their backs on him and refused to ever help the other souls upon the earth ever again. It was following this that the lord chose to place strong souls from another world and another time onto the earth. On the planet he placed dragons. These beasts were of equal intelligence to the other souls, though they had learnt all life's lessons and had become guardians of the worlds. They were powerful beings; their power almost matched that of the great lord himself. Yet they did not abuse this power. They were wise and knew that the best way of life was the way of peace.

The other souls upon the earth were fascinated by the dragons. They thought of them as a gift from the heavens, and instead of learning from them, they chose to own them as if they were common mules. The dragons were contempt to live like this in the hope that one day the beings of the earth would learn their mistake. However they did not. They felt that because the dragons were subdued beings, they were no more intelligent than the other animals. Here they made their biggest mistake. The three races of the earth began to take claim upon the dragons and name them as their own. A war was about to rage.

The elves sought out the dragons for the ability to use magic; they were the only race that saw the intelligence behind the dragon's dark eyes. The dwarves sought the dragons for the teeth and claws, they wished to use the dragons to overcome the elves and return to the land beyond their mountain tunnels. The humans wanted the dragons for the vast amount of flesh. They wished to dine upon the dragons and use their hide as clothes.

The dragons sensed a war approaching and chose to go into hiding, hoping this would solve the matter. They hid beyond the seas, in the dark forests, and on the highest peaks of the most secluded mountains. The races of the earth then began to blame each other for the loss of the dragons, and so over time the hate built yet the reasons were forgotten. Thousands of years past and still the races had not made up their differences or learnt the lessons of life. So they continued going no where in their existence and they slowly forgot about the creator, they even forgot the reasons they were there.

This infuriated the creator and he thought that the world in which he had created was no longer his own. It was then that he created a soul that had enough power to save the entire planet and its race's. This one soul had enough magic to save all the souls the creator had placed upon the earth. Yet there was a flaw in the plan that the lord did not foresee, although the soul had the power to save the earth, they had the power to destroy it too.

CHAPTER 2

Escape From The Gallows

"Freedom is something we all strive for, that feeling of being fully able to do as we wish and go where we please; but does true freedom not come from within, freedom from negative emotions such as fear, rage, and hate; freedom from mental attachments such as promises and ties to others. Does this not mean that all the time we are in love we are not free? All the time that we are surrounded by those we care for, we will always be tied to making them happy. However is this not all freedom of choice, or are our emotions towards others not already pre-planned by someone of a higher power and therefore uncontrollable by us?"

KAYLIN WAS SITTING in the courtyard outside the castle looking out across the grounds, sedately sipping a glass of rich red wine, made from the ripest grapes from the castles vineyard. He was enjoying the warm breeze across his face and he listened to the soft whispering of the wind. It seemed to be saying something but he could not quite make out what. He listened harder. Could he really have heard that? "Listen". He glanced around to see if there was someone around, however the courtyard was silent and empty from other beings. He listened again. "A threat approaches". Kaylin looked round again, but still he was quite alone. He shook his head and shrugged to himself. It must be the pressure of the job, he thought to himself, after all there was not a person on the earth more important than himself, after all he was king.

He remained there a while longer. He sat on the small wall that surrounded a water fall which was situated in the centre of the courtyard. Kaylin pondered his kingdom and thought himself a wonderful king. This is not untrue, for in all his time as king, a war had not raged, there had been no hangings and all in all life was rather quiet. It had been a good harvest this year and there had been no natural disasters to date. Of course he knew that the last two were not his doing but of course it made him even more of a successful king. The final thing that added to his rather splendid mood was the rather fine weather they were having.

Kaylin looked up at the sky and noticed it turning a light shade of lilac. Ah, time for tea, he thought to himself. He slowly rose from his sitting position and made his way through the tall marble pillars and towards the castle doors. He was just about to proceed indoors when he heard a shout from behind him.

"King Kaylin, sir, your highness! We have a prisoner," a young man with blonde hair tied back in a pony tail came running across the courtyard. He could have been no older than sixteen. He stopped in front of Kaylin breathing heavily.

Stupid boy, thought Kaylin. Why run it only makes you out of breath.

"Was it necessary to bring that to my attention? Could you not have told the head guard on duty? Honestly its tea time."

"I did sir, only he told me to alert you and ask you to come down to the cells where the prisoner is being held."

"Why must I take time out of my very hectic schedule just to see a prisoner?"

"Erm," the young boy seemed to be contemplating this answer. "Because Tarlin believes that this prisoner needs your immediate attention sir."

Kaylin thought for a while, torn between the investigation of this prisoner and the supper that awaited him in the castle dinning hall. "Fine," he muttered. "Take me to this prisoner."

The boy made a quick bow and turned back the way he had come and led the king out of the courtyard and down a lane leading in to the heart of the city. The lane was cobbled with light colored stones that had now turned a dirty brown after years of filth being thrown out onto the street. Only a short way down the lane the boy turned right down a darker lane that then opened up onto a high street. The street consisted of many stone houses that were slowly dilapidating. Out side these houses were wooden stalls. They had been emptied of their owners stock and stood bare upon the street. The king and the boy continued to the end of the street. It was here that they entered a large dark stoned building that represented a cave. It was only one storey for the cells were underground. The king proceeded down a series of cold, damp steps. In front of him now were a number of dark cells constructed of black iron bars. In most of the cells were large well wielded chains. These were apparently to chain up prisoners should they try to escape; not that we need them, thought Kaylin.

Kaylin looked very out of place here in the dim, damp, dark prison. It seemed that he was the only source of color in the entire room. He wore a cloak of deep purple, and the rest of his attire was completely white.

A well built man then strode round the corner at the end of the line of cells and approached Kaylin.

"Evening sir, I am glad to see that you felt the urgency of our meeting and came at my request." He said in a deep and powerful voice that, even though, seemed to contain no threat.

"Well I would rather be relishing myself with my supper," Retorted the King.

"Ah, yes quite sir." Came the reply.

"Well then Tarlin where is this prisoner and what have they done?"

Tarlin paused for a moment then answered, "She is down in the last cell at the moment sire, and we currently have her restrained, though she has proved difficult. I have now lost three of my best men." The king looked shocked at this. In all his time as king there had never been a murder let alone three. After all he was the greatest king there had ever been, nothing could ever go wrong under his rule.

"We have arrested her for; the destruction of seven small villages surrounding the castle, counting almost three thousand deaths, treason, for we have evidence she was planning to attack you sire, impersonating a guard in an attempt to gain access to the castle, thievery, vandalism by fire, and slander." Once again the king failed to hide his surprise at the list of crimes.

"We found her in possession of an ancient yet magnificent blade that is obviously stolen, a bow, quiver and arrows also of fine quality which I also believe to be stolen and a most peculiar necklace with a tooth pendant." Tarlin finished with a questioning note in his voice. "It is a most strange pendant sire, the shape of the tooth, I have seen nothing like it."

"May I see it?" asked Kaylin.

"Oh no sire, what makes it more peculiar is that no one can touch it?" Kaylin looked questioningly at the guard. "When ever anyone touches it, it burns them, I have seen many of my men attempt to take it from her and they are all thrown away from her covered in severe burns, it is like they have walked through flame sir." Tarlin paused, "could it be magic?" Tarlin knew that to mention anything unordinary was risky, though he thought that the king should know the truth before he met this evil prisoner.

"Magic!" yelled the king, "I will not hear of such rubbish you are lucky I don't cut out your tongue. There is no such thing! Fairy tales if you must, stories for children. But I will not have that sort of rubbish mentioned in my presence, or anyone else's for that matter. Now take me to this prisoner."

Tarlin looked away from the king, turned and walked down to the end of the corridor of cells. He gestured towards the cell in which the captive was being held.

Kaylin could not believe what he saw. Five grown men were struggling to hold down a young woman no older than eighteen. She caught the king's gaze and stared into his eyes. He glanced back, taking in her features. She had long brown hair that was sleek and well kept, she had high cheek bones and her features were well proportioned. But what caught Kaylin's attention was her eyes. Her right eye was a dark brown, yet her left eye was pitch black. Upon her eye was a vivid red scar. It ran from just above her eyebrow to just below her cheek bone.

Kaylin stared into her mad eyes. The girl fought against the chains. The five guards heaved on the metal chains with all their force and still were only just managing to hold her back. With one last effort the girl lunged towards the king, the chains being wrenched out of the guards hands. Kaylin went to step back, though the girl stopped, righted herself and stood calmly in front of him.

He stared at the spectacular prisoner and waited for speech, however none came, she just continued to hold his gaze.

The guards stood transfixed, unable to move forward and grab the chains laid upon the floor which were still bound heavily around the girl's wrists and ankles. Tarlin gave the king a nervous look but made no move to re-contain the prisoner.

"I hear," said the king with as much authority as possible, "that you have been causing havoc in my kingdom." Kaylin did not expect her to speak, however as he continued to stare into her face he heard a voice in the back of his mind. He rechecked the girls face to make sure she had not spoken; she hadn't. The king pushed the mumbling in his head to one side and put it down to the stress of the job. "What is your name?" He asked as if he was speaking to a small child.

I will not be spoken to like some common fool. This time the king was sure, he was hearing voices in his head. To the on looking guards the king became a pale shade of grey and he appeared to have lost his overpowering demeanor.

You are a young fool, Came the voice again. *I will answer you my name if you will answer me yours?*

The king thought little about this question, and answered immediately. "My name is Kaylin," he said out loud, it had not occurred to him that the prisoner could hear him quite well in is head and had heard the answer even before he had spoken it.

You may address me by the name of Rose, many do. The king, all of a sudden, managed to gather together his courage. "What are you? Why are you here? How have you caused so much death in my kingdom? How are you talking to me in my mind?" This all exploded rather rapidly from the king's mouth, so fast in fact that it was hard to make the sentence out to contain individual words. The guards of course were all now incredibly confused due to the fact that they had heard no speech from Rose, and they now wondered if the pressure of the job was finally getting to the king. Rose however understood his meaning perfectly for she had seen the thought being created in his mind and had heard the questions before it had even left his tongue.

I feel that what are you is rather a harsh thing to say, yet I shall answer it. I am a living being just like you, surely a king as wise as you can see that. I am here because I have a date with a very important person in which I have not had the pleasure of seeing for a terribly long time. Your third question, if I remember rightly was, 'how have you caused so much death in my kingdom?' The deaths in which I caused were not entirely my fault. I was and still am under strict instructions from someone of higher authority than even you. I am unaware as to why those people had to be slaughtered; only that it was a very important task in which I had to undertake. As for your last question, I believe it is possible for anyone to communicate through telepathy, else how would animals and dragons communicate?

The king had taken the majority of this quite well, however at the mention of dragons his heart skipped a beat and the color that had earlier vanished from his face had now rapidly returned.

"Dragons!" His voice had now become a higher pitch than usual; he seemed to notice this as he put his hand to his throat and winced as though it caused him physical pain. "There are no such creatures as dragons, they are myth. Had they existed then they would have soon been killed due to their viciousness and monstrous tendencies."

Really, said Rose deep from within the king's mind. *So you don't believe in dragons?*

"Of course I bloody well don't. And you do I suppose? You think that there are creatures out there, deep in hiding that can breathe fire, control the elements, read minds and have the equal intellect of us human beings?"

That's exactly what I believe.

"Then I have to disagree with you and say that you are completely bonkers. I am afraid to have to break this to you but dragons do not exist. They are mere myth, fables, and fairy tales."

I have a close friend that I think would strongly disagree with you. For you see I don't just think that dragons are real, I know that they are.

"Ha," came the king's reply. "If you can show me a dragon I will surrender to you my entire kingdom." Kaylin let out a hearty laugh.

Rose did not reply to this, but a dark, sinister smirk appeared on her face.

The guards all of a sudden seemed to wake from a trance. They lunged towards the chains and proceeded to wrestle Rose to the ground. This time however she did not protest, she just allowed her self to be dragged across the rough cobbled floor and in to the corner of the cell where she was finally chained to the wall.

The king watched the proceedings before turning to Tarlin. "The gallows, tomorrow at noon. Let us be rid of this foul, demented beast."

• •

Rose remained in the dark, damp cell for the rest of the night, and the following morning. She was quite content even though it was only hours before she was to face her end, short drop and a sudden stop. It did not seem to faze her at all, even perhaps as though this sort of thing was experienced every day.

When the sun was high in the light blue sky ten guards came to escort her to the gallows. They were heavily armed with bows and swords. However these were not needed as Rose came sedately and walked calmly to the town square were she was to be hung. The high street that she walked through was full of peasants that booed and hissed as she went passed. They looked weary and were in general worse for wear. They all appeared rather down trodden, in fact it seemed to Rose as if they were barely even human. She strode past them, her head held high. She ignored their angry glares and shouts of abuse. The guards held her strong iron chains fast, wondering whether she was planning to escape. Even as she made her way out on to the town square she made no attempt of escape. The town square was usually used for markets and trades men, and perhaps the occasional performance. Now however it contained a large wooden stage. Upon the top of the platform was a wooden bar, the one in which Rose would hang from.

Still Rose made no move to attempt an escape, she merely allowed the guards to escort her up the wooden steps leading to the platform. The guards removed the chains and stepped away from their prisoner. They placed themselves in a line at the back of the stage where they were correctly positioned to use their bows and arrows should Rose try to flee.

King Kaylin stepped out from behind the stage and addressed the awaiting crowd. Today he was dressed in a red cloak with a black tunic and leggings. He wore a golden belt that glistened in the afternoon sunlight. A golden crown perched upon his head encrusted with red and blue gems.

"Ladies and gentlemen," began the king. "You are here today to witness the hanging of a criminal under the name of Rose. The accused has been convicted of: the destruction of seven small villages surrounding the castle, counting almost three thousand deaths, treason, impersonating a guard in an attempt to gain access to the castle, thievery, and vandalism by fire, and slander. Here we have," Kaylin gestured towards a finely made broad sword with red and black gems inlaid upon the hilt, the sheath also of a remarkable standard and also being decorated with red and black gems, and a fine delicate bow with a quiver containing arrows made from elm wood and swan feathers. "For auction the items in which you see before me. They shall be sold after the hanging. Now we shall proceed." Kaylin nodded to a hunch backed man dressed from head to toe in black. All that could be seen were his green eyes beneath his black hood. Kaylin stepped to the side of the platform and watched the proceedings.

The executioner shuffled towards Rose and tentatively placed the rope around her neck. He grumbled quietly before proceeding to a large wooden handle beside her. The crowd were on edge, hanging upon the sound of the now existent drum roll in which was coming from the back of the town square behind the sea of people. All the executioner had to do was pull the leaver and the floor beneath Rose would fall, causing her to fall to her death. However the executioner paused. In the distance came a rumbling so deep it resembled thunder. The crowd took their eyes of Rose and looked about themselves. Again came the roar, closer this time. It was a rough grumbling sound that hit the very souls of the people assembled in the town. The drum roll stopped as the drummers gazed up at the sky searching for the cause of the noise.

Suddenly from deep within the crowd came a gasp. "Look up there." People followed the direction of a finger pointing from within the mass of people. This was followed by more gasps. Everyone now had taken their eyes off of Rose and was staring at the same spot in the sky. Far in the distance, only a speck was visible, and it could easily have been assumed that it could have been a bird. Again came the tremendous roar that seemed to echo around the town square causing it to shake. The bird grew nearer. It appeared to be of a black and red color. Closer still drew the bird, and still the town shook with the deafening roar. Then most unexpectedly a jet of red flame erupted from the creature's mouth. People began to scream and turned to flee from the town square. Others stood transfixed gazing at the beast that was now so close its features were now clearly distinguishable.

"Dragon," whispered the king. He spun to face Rose who through all the exciting proceedings had not moved at all. She gazed up at the sky following the progress of the dragon. The beast roared again this time causing the ground to shake, sending people running in all directions. With many people having fled this now left the gigantic beast with enough room to land. It hovered twenty feet above the ground before landing gently upon it back legs, and proceeding to crash his front legs upon the cobbled street. Again the dragon roared causing a whirling wind that sent debris flying around the town square. It allowed another jet of flame to burst from its mouth causing the wooden platform to erupt in a mass of fire. At this point, the guards, executioner, king and Rose leapt away from the flames. In the split second before the dragon had conjured the fire Rose had pulled herself from the noose and snatched her belongings from the front of the stage.

As the platform burnt the town square erupted into chaos. Women were screaming, children crying and people parted from their family and friends. Rose ran stealthily up to the dragon, crawled up its leg and leapt gracefully onto its back between two spikes. The girl seemed completely at home sat astride the dragon, as though it was the most comfortable place she could be.

With one swift movement of her right hand the flames upon the platform disappeared leaving only a burnt out mass of blackened wood and ash. The remainder of the crowd, with shock, turned to face the girl and the dragon.

"Shoot her!" Yelled Kaylin, pointing towards the thirty foot dragon and its rider. The guards stood for a moment before fixing arrow to bow. They then sent their arrows flying towards Rose, only to be deflected by a flick of her wrist. Many of the arrows were embedded into the flesh of some of the peasants; their screams pierced the air and echoed around the town square. Kaylin ground his teeth and glared at Rose.

"Now do you believe in dragons," cried Rose over the noise of the screaming crowd. She let out a loud cackle at his angry yet astonished expression.

Kaylin continued to grind his teeth unable to think of anything which would help the situation. He glanced up at the magnificent dragon. Its body was a livid blood red with black stripes. The tines that ran from the tip of its broad stoat nose to the tip of its long snake like tail were also black and were refined in to razor sharp points. It claws dug into the cobble stoned street leaving large gash marks. It snaked its head round to look directly at Kaylin. Its eyes were a dark black with no hint of color, yet they held an immense beauty, what appeared to be an entrance to its soul, and it seemed that no matter how long you gazed into its eyes you would always learn something new for they held a wisdom, a wisdom in which no other creature or being could ever have mastered.

You may keep your kingdom, Rose and I have no need or want of it. But heed my words human, there are dragons, there are dwarves and elves too, in fact a lot more than just what you see is out there too. Perhaps you could take it upon yourself to find these other races and meet with them. Maybe old feuds can be forgotten. Perhaps. Just remember there is more to this world than meets the eye. Just listen to your soul. I am a dragon, so heed my words.

Kaylin continued to stare at the dragon. It had spoken to him, gave him advice. Should he really take the advice of a dragon? The beast leapt into the air, twisting as it went to face the direction it had come. It rose in the air rapidly, its large wings beating the sky in a slow steady rhythm.

Heed my words Kaylin, we shall meet again!

CHAPTER 3

Sarabie

"That bright star high up in the sky, symbolizes that small light at the end of the tunnel, that ray of hope in the darkness; that small chance that even in the hardest of times, things will get better."

NOW WE WILL go back a few years to a time when things were far different than the time in which our main tale is told. In the heart of the Garathien kingdom stood a grand castle of white marble; a castle so marvelous that it would in fact not look too out of place in heaven. Rays of bright yellow sunlight seemed to always shine down upon the castle as if the angels themselves were gazing down upon it making sure no harm came to the dwelling or those who dwelled within it. Of course night would fall and the sun would sink into the horizon, yet still light would fall upon the castle; even on the cloudiest of nights the moon would shine through and enlighten the grand marble building. Four towers rose from each corner of the castle and the entrance was guarded by two large golden dragons. The golden beasts stood proud over the marble steps glowering down upon those who dared enter the fantastic building and taint its beauty with their presence. Beyond the marble steps and the intimidating dragons stood huge golden doors lined with glittering red rubies. As one passed through these grand doors, it was then that the atmosphere changed from being awed by the magnificent beauty of the exterior of the castle, to be shadowed by a suppressing feeling of dread and foreboding. It was as though all the joy had been sapped from the atmosphere within the castle and all was left was the dry and bitter taste of hate and anger. The air was heavy with a depressing oppression and it was as though no hope could possibly exist in any shape or form.

The large entrance hall of the castle was empty and echoey. It seemed full of lost ghosts searching for a way to escape their evil torment of being trapped within the castles walls.

The castle was home to the king and queen of Garathien and their young son, Karbith. To all onlookers the three appeared happy and carefree. However their servants knew different, for although it was arranged for Karbith to be next in line to the throne, he was not the heir. Hidden away in the furthest, darkest corridor of the castle was the eldest descendant of the king and the queen.

The girl curled in the corner of the ill lit room held a royal grace, an immense beauty that seemed to radiate from her like rays of sunlight. She seemed ill suited to her surroundings; the room was damp and dark, and smelt badly of mould and stale urine. The room had a small window with wrought iron bars across it. It allowed little light into the room as it was late in the evening. The girl was clothed in filthy rags, her hair matted and uncared for. Yet this failed to flaw her good looks.

She gazed out of the window and sang quietly to herself,

> *"Is there any one who knows me*
> *Do they all know who I could be*
> *How can I be so insecure*
> *How can I be so lost*
> *Should change the way I am*
> *Or should I carry on in darkness*
> *When all around me I see black*
> *Where is the light to guide me*
> *Is there some one out there who will find me."*

From outside the room came footsteps, after a short time the door opened and a middle aged woman walked in carrying a wooden dish containing a foul looking soup. The woman was well dressed; she wore a lilac dress which was heavily frilled. Her hair was a light blonde which was neatly plaited and bound by a ribbon. She approached the young girl in the corner tentatively, as though the girl may suddenly pounce and attack. However the girl seemed completely oblivious to the woman in the room, and she continued to gaze out of the window singing quietly under her breath.

"Sarabie?" The girl seemed to awake as if from a daydream and glanced up at her mother.

"This all the food I could scrape without your father noticing." The woman approached her daughter and placed the dish on the dirt covered floor. The woman crouched down beside the girl and waited for her to speak, how ever Sarabie turned away from her mother and chose to gaze at the scene outside the window. Sarabie had spent many years staring out of that very window, wondering how it would feel to run about the grass, climb the great old oak, and to swim in the stream that she could hear if all was quiet and she listened very hard. Sarabie could picture the stream now in her mind; bright clear water with pink lilies dotted about its surface, a rough bank of golden sand about the waters edge, and just a small way down stream there was the most magnificent grand old willow tree that stood guard over the ever peaceful stream that seemed touched by no one.

"It is not my choice for you to remain in here. You know your father."

"He is no father of mine!" retorted Sarabie.

"Mmm, I am sorry for the way you have been treated." Sarabie's mother knelt by her side and placed the bowl of soup on the dirt covered floor next to her. She then proceeded to place her hand on Sarabie's arm. Immediately the young girl shied away from her mothers touch and she shuffled backwards so that her back was now firmly against the wall below the window.

"Then do something about it Sky." Sarabie could only have been about thirteen; however the use of her mothers name rather than her title seemed to hurt more than any physical blow; along with of course Sarabie's rejection to her subtle hand gesture.

"Your right dear, I should have done this long ago." She paused as if she was gathering the strength to speak. "I am going to help you escape. The way in which your father has treated you since the birth of

Karbith has been despicable, and I as your mother should have put a stop to it immediately.

Later on tonight your father is leaving for a meeting with someone called Christith, this will be your only chance to escape; therefore we must make sure that we have a strong plan. I am sure you understand that if either of us is caught then that will be the end. Once your father, Gaston has left you will have about an hour to get as far away from the castle as possible. However before you leave the castle I wish you to go down to the treasury and take a large red gem in the shape of an egg. I want you to listen carefully to what I have to say next, because it is this gem that your father guards so secretively. To him that stone is worth a million lives; to him no money could buy this gem, a price could not be lain upon it. However the stone does not belong to him; I was given it to give to you on your thirteenth birthday, which of course is today." Sarabie had been completely unaware that it was her birthday, for she had spent over half of her life in this dark cell deep beneath the castle. "This egg is of great importance. Guard it with your life, and it will guard your life with its. With it I want you to flee to the forests to the north. Keep the largest mountain peak directly in front of you and you will come to a large mound made of limestone, there you will meet a friend of mine. He will look after you from then on."

"Why is this red stone so important?"

"You will find out, just listen to your soul. I will leave the door unlocked, so when the moon is directly above your window you must flee, but remember take the red stone with you." Sky rose and walked to the door, "Remember your father is king, and he will do what ever it takes to cover up your existence so don't get caught." Sky took one last look at her daughter and left the cell leaving the door slightly ajar.

Now although Sarabie had spent the majority of her years in this dark cell, it could definatly not have be said that the girl lacked intelligence. She seemed to know things; as in things that she should not or could not have known by theory. Therefore it was questionable as to whether she really was intelligent or whether she had the capability of using some other, more supernatural power. Yet whether she was using intellect or some psychic power, Sarabie knew that this was the last time she would ever see her mother, alive. Sarabie knew that for her mother to follow her to the great mountain would surely leave a trail for her father to follow; although Sarabie did doubt greatly that she would be able to accomplish the mission herself.

Sarabie watched the cell door close and wished that her mother could have stayed just a moment longer; just long enough for Sarabie to say, "I love you." After all the young girl knew well of the predicament within the family and therefore understood that all problems within the castle stemmed from her father. Sarabie longed to have been able to spend her childhood years with her mother; just like all other normal children. She had not chosen to be some royal princess, Sarabie would have given up all the riches in the world just to have spent some more time with her mother, and perhaps just enjoy the sunshine together. Instead the young girl knew that her childhood years were long gone, and they would never return to her, her mother too.

Sarabie watched the moon drift slowly across the black sky. She suddenly felt like there was a light at the end of the tunnel, a small ray of hope. Even though she would no longer see her mother, Sarabie knew that this was her best chance at a better life. No more daily beatings from her father, no more listening to the laughter of Karbith as he skipped down the corridor completely unaware that he had an older sister who was in fact sat only a few yards away on the other side of a door.

As the moon drew parallel with the window she rose slowly and approached the door. It had been seven years since she had left the dark room, yet she remembered the layout of the castle well, for all her daydreams consisted of her creeping through the castle halls and escaping this living hell. She listened hard and pushed the door open. Sarabie tentatively poked her head around the door frame and examined the corridor; it was the same as it had been seven years ago. She turned left and followed the corridor round and crept down the stairs. Sarabie felt weak from lack of nutrition, however she did not let this affect her, and she gathered her strength and opened the door at the bottom of the staircase. Once again the corridor was deserted. She thought briefly of the whereabouts of the treasury, and then proceeded left. She came to a large set of oak doors and pushed them open. The room was full of gold and silver objects, jewels and stones. Sarabie did not find it hard to seek what she was looking for. The red stone caught her attention immediately and even though she had been told to collect the stone, she felt that had she not been told what it looked like she would have chosen it anyway.

She approached the stone with care, and reluctant to damage it picked it up with caution. Beneath her touch the stone began to glow. A bright white light seemed to erupt from the stone and with a high pitch screech the stone split. Sarabie immediately dropped the stone. It hit the ground and shattered. Pieces flew across the room leaving only the white light gleaming upon the floor. The light began to grow rapidly and soon it filled the whole room. Sarabie shielded her eyes and turned away from the light. Almost as quickly as it had appeared it vanished. Sarabie turned to look at the remains of the stone; however none was left except for a small winged lizard standing at around twelve inches tall. It hiccupped and let out a small wisp of smoke. Sarabie glanced around her but still the castle was completely still. She turned to face the dragon. It gazed up at her, its eyes a dark black, its hide a livid red. As the girl looked at the dragon she noticed that the dragon had grown, it was now the size of a large dog. Sarabie stepped backwards yet walked directly into something. She went to turn around yet found her self restricted as a hand grasped her throat. It pushed hard and Sarabie struggled to catch her breath. "So you thought you could escape from me child!" Sarabie broke free from her fathers grip and spun to face him. "I knew when your mother asked to check on you before we left that she was planning something. Your are an evil child that deserved the treatment you received," his voice now turned into a harsh whisper, "You aren't worth the air you breath, nor are you worthy of the name you were given. You are now going to receive the same fate as your stupid mother." Sarabie's father drew a sword from a sheath belted it to his waist. He brought the sword level with his shoulder and was about to land the final blow when a jet of flame came soaring over Sarabie's shoulder and hit her father square in the face. He let out a soul piercing scream and dropped the sword. Sarabie grabbed the sword and fled from the castle. She crossed the entrance hall at an incredible speed, the sword slowing her down very little. After exiting the castle through large mahogany doors, Sarabie turned to look at it one last time. Then she raced across the well pruned lawns, but then she felt a piercing pain in her shoulder. She collapsed hitting the ground hard. She could feel the ground vibrating beneath her as someone approached. She felt herself being dragged off of the ground and placed on to her own feet that seemed barely able to support her weight. She saw before her once again her father, this time however his face was raw and weeping, having had all of the flesh burnt off. He growled before wrenching the arrow from Sarabie's back. She felt the muscles tear as a river of blood flowed down her back. "YOU DARE TO ESCAPE FROM ME AND YOU DARE TO STEAL MY SWORD, MY SWORD!" he screamed in to her face, his eyes mad with anger. He snatched the sword from the ground and drove it hard through Sarabie's stomach, she gasped as breath escaped her before her body collapsed as the blade was withdrawn. Although her vision was failing her she was sure that she had seen an overgrown red lizard attack her father before lifting her from the ground in its large talons, raising itself in to the air and taking flight towards the forest to the north.

It's alright your safe now.

. . . .

Sarabie awoke to find herself stiff and sore, she could barely move. She opened her eyes a crack and tried to figure out where she was. At first the light stung her eyes slightly and she noted that she was in a well light cave made of white stone. She seemed to be laid upon a rough woolen blanket, though she wasn't sure. Sarabie couldn't make out her surroundings in much detail as she was unable to turn her head. She then found that her stomach and shoulder had been bound in cloth and felt pain in neither area. Although Sarabie was unsure of how she had ended up in this current predicament, she did distinctly remember horrific pain in both her shoulder and her stomach, however now there was none.

"Here, drink this." A young face then appeared within in Sarabie's line of vision. He had a well proportioned face and looked more feline than human, although his features were masculine. He had short brown hair that was extremely scruffy with a fringe that hung limply across his face. He had deep brown eyes that were warm and comforting. The man knelt beside her and raised a wooden cup to her lips, Sarabie allowed the cool liquid to run down the back of her throat, it was then that she appreciated how thirsty she had been. The water soothed her burning throat; it felt to her as if her through consisted of burning coals that chilled the instant that they were hit by the water. Once she had drunk her fill, Sarabie brought herself up onto her elbows, though could not muster the energy to lift herself upright.

"Here, I will help you." The man placed his hands beneath her arms and raised her up slowly leaning her against the wall. "I have healed the two stab wounds, though you have been on the edge of death for a long time now so you will feel weak for a while until we can get your strength up." The young man reassured her with a grin. "My name is Laylan; I was contacted by your mother a while ago about helping you to escape. I will however tell you that I have been meaning to rescue you from that horrid castle for some time. I was unaware until a month ago of how you were being treated, had I known sooner I would have brought you back to where you belong."

Sarabie gazed curiously at Laylan trying to figure out if he was talking sense and she was failing to understand due to her injury or he was talking total utter rubbish that could be made neither heads nor tails of by anyone. "What do you mean, where I belong?"

"Elvendin; the great forest, the home of the elves." Laylan's reply to Sarabie's question was answered by an even more confused glare.

"Now since you were born there has been a lot of speculation amongst my people about you. Know however this will end for the truth is here; in fact it's sitting right outside this very cave." Laylan turned to face the entrance of the cave. Through the caves mouth walked the most magnificent beast Sarabie had ever seen. It had bright red scales that glistened like crystals, razor sharp claws and tines across its back, its head was triangular in shape with large fangs the size of a persons wrist. It stood at around six feet tall at its back. Its long neck snaked into the cave, followed by its body, then tail. The dragon turned to look at Sarabie; it had pitch black eyes that appeared bottom less, as if you could dive right into the creature's soul.

Good afternoon. Sarabie heard the voice in her head; she thought about it briefly then replied,

I can speak back to you in my head, right?

Yes you can, this is the art of telepathy, and it is the way in which all animals communicate.

Sarabie looked into the dragons eyes. *Do you have a name?* Asked Sarabie.

Not as yet, it is up to you to name me. I have been born to you. Something about you made my egg split, therefore the lord has asked us to watch over each other, and so it will be. Dragons hatch for nothing else but their mothers touch, however the lord gave me not to a dragon; he gave me to you, as you were given to me. You are free to give me any name you chose, well as long as I agree to it.

Sarabie considered the red dragon for a moment. For the period in which the girl and the dragon were conversing, Laylan remained in a respectful silence, seemingly understanding what the pair were undergoing.

Nenamis, Niver Nenamis, said Sarabie deep with in her mind. Immediately she felt the dragons content with the name. It felt strange to Sarabie to feel someone else's emotions, to see in to someone else's mind. In fact it felt completely alien to Sarabie to be feeling joy. She looked deep it to Nenamis's eyes and felt safe, he had saved her life, for no other reason apart from that he wanted her alive. Nenamis turned away from Sarabie and stalked outside where he had more room. She watched him go, wanting him to stay. However even though he was now thirty or so meters away, she could still feel his conscious within hers. This seemed to comfort Sarabie, she did not feel alone for the first time in her life, for the first time she had a friend.

After a while Sarabie remembered that there was someone else in the cave with her. Feeling slightly more alive after talking to Nenamis she sat herself up and turned to face Laylan.

"We must leave soon, we can not linger here to long there are people looking for you. We must take you into the forest amongst my people where we can care for you until you can fend for yourself."

"Who are your people? Where are we going? Why is my safety so important?"

"You have much to learn. A lot rests on your shoulders, and I am ashamed to have to ask so much of someone so young. However to achieve what we must, your training must begin now, you and your dragon have been long awaited. I am not the one to explain every thing to you. My people live deep within the forest, protected by various enchantments so that we are undetected by the king of men. We do not live amongst the race of humans for we have many differences, for we are elves. We believe in living in harmony with the world and the creatures on it. However dwarves and men disagree, this is where you come in. You are a gift from the lord. We elves need your help to teach the people of the world how to live in peace. Now we must go, I believe that your dragon will carry you. As for me, well I shall run beneath you, another thing I do hope is that you are not scared of heights, for being partners with a dragon means you will spend a lot of time off the ground."

"Just one more thing," said Sarabie. "What must I learn?"

"Many things, magic, swordsmanship, archery and how to control your mind. The world is at war Sarabie, and you are our only hope."

CHAPTER 4

Old Friends

"It is black because it has nothing left
No joyous emotions or happy memories
All it has left is evil, sadness and malice
These emotions have darkened its heart
And drowned all color from its soul
It is black to show its sourful outlook on life
Its meager existence
It is black to show what is after life
As once life is done evil takes over
And you move on to a place
That has no hope, no love
And all that is left is the same blackness of the Rose
And the same evil and hate that it has seen in life
An admired beauty that is filled with total blackness
A flower that has grown from the bush of hell"

ROSE SAT ON the highest hill in the green open valley. This was her favorite place to watch the world go by. She seemed to have the amazing ability to be able to sit on the edge of the valley, at its highest point for days on end with no need for food or water. This was one of the things that puzzled many of the folk that attempted to follow Rose in her many movements across the kingdom; she never needed to rest or replenish herself. This of course made her untouchable, she could not be tracked over distances and she could never be beaten in a fight as she never tired. This of course then caused people to contemplate her being super human. There was also the contemplation about as to whether or not she was mortal; after all she had seemed to age very little over the past few years.

Rose, since her escape from the gallows, the common folk had become completely transfixed by her and often spent the majority of their day discussing whether or not she was an alien from another planet, or if she was some form of demon sent from the underworld to destroy the Earth and have vengeance upon the lord. However the truth was something that the common folk of the kingdom were incredibly unlikely to ever know.

Rose gazed upon the grassy valley, its immense beauty captivating her, the sunlight filling the hollow of the land causing it to seemingly glow. It was apparent that Rose was agitated and nervous. She felt completely out of place, as though she were a black dot on a white background, the black sheep of the flock. The wind was soft upon her face, it whispered to her; however she ignored it and continued to gaze blankly across the countryside. The warmth of the suns rays bore down to the bottom of her soul, and seemed to finally raise her from a deep trance. Rose turned and faced the dragon sat beside her.

I am sorry for what I did, Thalayli.

Mmm, its ok, if there is one thing that I have learnt from spending all these years with you, it is to expect the unexpected. The pair conversed telepathically; even so the dragon's voice was deep and rough, yet wise as though it held all the knowledge of the world and beyond.

Well, would life not be boring if we played by the rules? Came Rose's reply.

If you played by the rules you mean? However that which I wish to know, is why you went through so much trouble to just make my presence known? Could you not have simply told him or perhaps just shown him a memory. Were the murders necessary, after all you know how much I object to the killing of innocent people; however due to the nature of our bond I seem to find it terribly hard to dissuade you from such ill crimes and injustices.

You know why I had to destroy the villages, I was under orders.

There was silence between them for a moment, before Thalayli answered; *I wish you would share with me what happened. It has created a wall between us. I will not judge you for what happened, or what you have to do, I just wish to know why, as currently I am finding your actions highly unethical.*

You know that I cannot tell you, I am sorry. Thalayli shook his extraordinarily large, magnificent head as yet another silence elapsed.

After a long period of companionship, Rose stood up and approached the dragon.

We must fly; there is someone I think we should meet.

I agree, I hear it on the wind, scent it on the breeze. A war is approaching and it is one that perhaps we can prevent.

Rubbish! I just fancy meeting an old friend. All this bloody talk of fate ect, you sound like the bloody elves. Now, let's get going. The great dragon seemed, to an onlooker, lift its shoulders in a shrugging motion as he simply accepted Rose's statement and put it down to her closed mind which did not seem to the dragon to be abnormal. After all, the human and dragon had been together many years now and therefore knew each other inside out and back to front. Although, Thalayli had noted a distinct change in Rose; he had put it down to a certain chapter of their life that Rose had sworn never to discuss. It was in fact a period in which they were not together; in fact it was a period that Thalayli did not even remember, yet it seemed to cover several years. However the dragon simply disregarded this as he had done with many other issues or discussions with Rose that were better off ignored; after all, Thalayli knew what Rose was capable off, and therefore chose not to push her over the line and tempt her darker more sinister side to appear.

And so it was that Rose leapt elegantly upon the grand beast; Thalayli then leapt mightily into the air and with one great swoop of his enormous wings, forgetting all of his woes as he disappeared in to the heavenous skies.

· ·

Dean and Jack were traipsing through the undergrowth of the dark forest. The forest was thick with oak and fir trees that seemed to tower over the pair as they painfully made their way. Thorns and nettles clawed at the men as they fought through the overgrown mass of greenery that seemed to envelop them making it difficult to stay true to their path. The pair were plainly dressed and carried only a sword each, otherwise they travelled light. They came to a clearing deep within the wood; it was here that they chose to rest for the evening.

"We will rest for a while; we must aim to be at Karbith's by morning." Jack looked at his brother and waited for his agreement.

"Ye, fine, whatever." Dean sat on the mossy earth and leant against a tree trunk. Jack sat himself beside Dean and together they remained in silence, just enjoying each others company.

It was not long before the pair had, in their drowsiness, fallen asleep. However they were completely unaware that they were currently being watched. Now crouched high above them was a young woman. She gazed down at them with a scornful look on her face, as though sleeping was a filthy habit that should be broken. The girl sat there for as long as the brothers lay together asleep. She did not look uncomfortable perched upon the branch of the tree; in fact she looked rather at home, as though there was no other place in the world in which she, herself could be more comfortable.

Dean shifted in his sleep, waking Jack as he did so. Jack noticed that the sky had turned a light red. The sun was now rising and the night was gone. Jack leapt to his feet and hurriedly awoke his brother. Dean also rapidly noted the suns position, and he also righted himself.

"We've got to go, now!" Said Dean, his voice filled with urgency. Jack nodded his head in reply, and turned to hurry off in the opposite direction of that in which they had entered the clearing. However, before he reached the trees the young girl that had been sat up in the tree, jumped gracefully down and landed elegantly before him with enough grace to quite easily outmatch that of a swan in water.

"Rose!" Jack took a step back and looked completely aghast at being stood in front of the girl. Dean leapt forward to stand beside his brother. "You're alive! Last time I heard you were dead!"

"Well, I feel quite alive," Rose pinched the skin on the back of her hand then proceeded, "Yep definitely alive, its funny you know, your not really classed as dead if you can still eat, feel and breath."

"You stopped feeling a long time ago, Rose," growled Dean. He gave her a hateful look that if possible would have caused Rose serious harm.

"Perhaps," she answered quite simply as though this came as no shock or offense to her in anyway.

"What brings you here?" asked Dean, trying to make his voice seem calm and unnerved.

"Why, I thought how nice it would be to come and see the pair of you, after all it has been a while, don't you think?"

"So y-you're not h-hear to k-kill us then?" stuttered Jack struggling to make his mouth form the correct shape for the words in which he wished to speak.

"Oh come on now, why would I do a horrid thing like that?" Rose smirked, seemingly finding it rather amusing that the two brothers were so scared of her. "Can't a girl visit her two eldest cousins every now and again?"

"What do you want Rose?" snapped Dean.

"Nothing, noting at all, I just wanted to see how you are that's all, is that a crime?"

"No, I suppose it is not. Though it is highly bewildering as to why you should suddenly take an interest in your cousin's, especially when they are delivering such an important message."

Dean said this with pride in his tone, however Rose just laughed and said; "You're still working for Karbith then? Well I suppose you must scrape a living some how. So what is this very important mission of yours then, of course it must be of great importance if Karbith has asked you two to fore fill it?"

It was now that Jack held his head high and proudly stated, "Well of course, Karbith chose the most skilled people for the job; the message had to be delivered with stealth so that it was not intercepted by the wrong person. After all Karbith meeting with the king is a very important matter, and could be terribly dangerous if someone else that wanted to sabotage the kings meeting, found out that it is being held at sunrise in three days. I mean you can see the dangers."

"Jack you bloody brainless buffoon. That message was top secret and you just blurted the whole bloody lot out to the one person who was not supposed to hear it. Were you last in line for brains or something? Grr am I surrounded by idiots?!"

"You know what Dean I think you are wrong, I for one am certainly no fool, as for Jack, well I refuse to pass judgment on him, and I fear that you have been greatly mislead and that you should perhaps take a better look at what is right in front of you, Dean. After all I can see everything, and I know that its been a long time since you took a look in the mirror; the reason being because you don't like what you see. That Dean, is because deep inside its not me you hate, or Jack; its yourself." Rose turned her gaze from Jack to Dean and glared at him hard. Dean averted his gaze rapidly, and chose to remain silent.

"Anyway, that information was of little use to me, I was in the presence of the king yesterday, so if I had wished to kill him, I could have done so then. Karbith, is another in which is not yet ready to die, so if you are worried about me committing murder then you have little, if nothing, to worry about; although I am still quite in the mood for old friends."

"Rose, is it really necessary for you to go. You will just cause trouble." Jack said this very tentatively.

"I will do exactly as I please, and no one is going to stop me. Also I have the distinct feeling that I am wanted there." Rose inclined her head slightly towards Dean as though acknowledging something that he had just said.

"Now, I will see you boys later." With that Rose turned, however she then looked back over her shoulder and said, "Oh and Dean, that thirst to prove yourself won't get you anywhere. In fact you will lose the only person who truly cares about you; and just remember that once something is truly broken, it can never be fixed. People can't be put back together like objects can." Rose then swiftly strode back into the woods, and was swallowed by darkness.

. . . .

Jack and Dean had left the forest far behind them now and were crossing a large meadow. At the bottom of the meadow, hidden beyond the brow of the hill was a small cottage. It was old yet well looked after, and was surrounded by a variety of different colored flowers and shrubs. Dean and Jack approached the cottage tentatively and knocked on the small oak door.

"You're late!" yelled a rough voice from inside. The two men opened the door and walked over the threshold. The interior of the cottage was dark and gloomy. It had the distinct air of having had something die within its walls. Jack and Dean walked through the small square hall into a living room on their left. Sat in a large padded chair was a young man of around eighteen. He had dark brown hair and brown eyes, his features were well defined and he had a royal grace about him. He rose from his chair and glared at the pair.

"Well?"

Dean shifted under his gaze. "She knows Karbith. She will be there, I know she will."

"Good, well done Dean. I will keep my promise to you, should of course Kaylin keep to what he promised." Dean bowed towards Karbith; however Jack turned fiercely towards his brother and gawped at him.

"You may now leave. Dean I will summon you when the time is right." Karbith nodded at the door and the two men left.

Outside Jack flew at his brother. "You lied to me!!"

"No I didn't, I just did not tell you."

"Why? We share every thing. You knew we were going to come across her and you didn't think to warn me. You lied, you lied to me and you don't even care! Why didn't you tell me?"

"It was my burden to bear."

"And what has Karbith promised you? You know not to trust him."

"I don't trust him, and never shall. However he has promised me great things, and now I will do his bidding willingly for that which he has promised. He has great plans Jack; maybe if you were more receptive to him he would have offered you the same. But it seems that I am of greater importance than you. You see, you are disposable, where as I am not." Jack stood gazing at his brother. Jack could not believe what he was hearing: they had spent their entire lives together, joined at the hip. In the twenty five years they had been together, never had they argued, and never had they insulted each other except for to take the piss out of one another. Jack now felt alone, as though he was facing the entire world with no one but himself. He felt lost for words, felt in shock. Jack took a step back and shook his head in disbelief.

"I'm not sorry Jack. You have been useful in the past, though now you have no further use. I don't need you any more. It has always been Dean and his stupid twin brother. Now it will be Dean, head of the largest army in Garathien, second in command to king Karbith. You will never bring me down again."

Jack still looked in shocked. He then took one last look at his brother and ran. He ran back into the forest, and tore at the shrubbery that attempted to slow him down. He then found himself in the same clearing where they had met Rose. It was here that Jack collapsed; he cried for hours. To him it felt as though his entire world was crashing down around him. He was surrounded by black; there was no light, no hope for him any more. Why was he so insignificant in the world that the only person he thought cared for him, had now abandoned him, and never really loved him at all?

CHAPTER 5

Next In Line To The Throne

"How far can we run before we tire?
How long will it take us to realize
That we just can't keep running
Because there will always come a time
When we can run no more
And we must turn around and fight
Because no one can run forever"

K AYLIN WORE A black woolen travelling cloak, the hood pulled tight over his head. He sat astride a grey war horse, which felt to him slightly on edge as the wind whistled around them and the rain stung their faces. He was flanked by eight guards, four travelled on foot, the others rode large bay stallions. The guards wore vivid red garments that stood out in their grim surroundings. Of course this uniform would be no good if perhaps there were was an attack, or if some one was trying to follow them, it would quite simply be a case of follow the red coats. However Kaylin, blinded by his ignorance and stupidity, failed to think of something like this and continued merrily through his simple plans.

On their right was a dark foreboding forest, on their left was an open plain that was covered in a grim marsh. The sky was a dark grey that gave little light to the troop of men travelling beneath it.

"How much further, Tarlin?" yelled the king over the roaring wind.

"Nearly there sire, half a league or so to go, we are meeting at the eastern edge of the forest."

They rode for another hour or so before two grey figures came into view. The two figures seemed deep in conversation, however as soon as the troop approached the pair became silent.

"Greetings Kaylin, I hope you had a good trip; I do hope you didn't find the weather to tiresome?" This was said by the shorter of the two men; he was around eighteen and was elegantly handsome.

"Thank you Karbith, the weather affected us little. Are we to discuss this here?" Kaylin, as typical of his nature got straight to the point.

"Yes, I don't think this should take too long. Of course you know why I have arranged this meeting with you?"

"Yes, I do. But are you sure you are ready for this? After all you are only eighteen, is this really the course you wish to take at your age?"

"It is, after all, my father is dead, and I am now of age to continue his work. Now it is time for you to step aside and allow me to take my throne, I am next in line!" This came across rather aggressively, which caught Kaylin of guard. The king paused for a moment then replied.

"Yes you are. I can not stop you; after all you are the previous king's only child. I hope you will run the kingdom as well as your father, if not better. But I ask only one thing of you; guard your people with your life." As Kaylin said this there came a roar from the skies. Next thing the men knew a large red and black dragon landed heavily beside them. The horses reared and bolted, leaving most of their riders sat on their backsides, in the cold wet mud. These men quickly rose and attempted to brush the dirt from themselves trying to make sure that they did not appear too unnerved by this experience.

Rose leapt from the dragons back and landed lightly beside Kaylin.

"We meet again Kaylin, I am sorry but I forgot to introduce you to my good friend, Thalayli. Unfortunately I was in rather a hurry last time we met due to the fact that you were attempting to hang me by the neck, from a beam." Kaylin grimaced and turned to Karbith.

"Why is she here?" he snapped.

"I thought it would be nice if she attended, after all she is a very big influence in the kingdom. In addition she has more power than any king ever has, or perhaps ever will. Wouldn't you agree, Rose?" Rose glared at Karbith, and then said, "I hope you have a happy time as king, but I must warn you, it will not last long."

"And how do you know this?" replied Karbith the new king.

"If I told you, I fear that it would be a total utter waste of my time, for you would not understand. I do have a question for you though, Karbith. Why did you want me here?"

"I thought that seeing as you think yourself so important, that perhaps you would like to be present at this meeting. However you now have me intrigued as to why you believe my reign as king to be short."

"Well quite simply the devil has been gathering people upon the earth to turn in to demons; he has also been raising an army down in hell which he intends to release upon the earth when the final gathering of the humans, elves, and dwarves occurs. As all the races congregate his army will bring terror upon the earth and destroy all who will not join him; that is of course if he has the patience to wait whilst everyone decides which side they wish to be on. Of course the Devil himself will not be present as he has far more important business to attend to such as tea parties with teddies; therefore his second in command will be in charge of the proceedings."

"Ok well I understand that you have no intention of telling me the truth so therefore I will drop my question and put your answer down to you having no real answer at all."

"Ye ok, whatever," At this point Rose moved in close to Karbith. "Look I have no wish to rule this kingdom, you may help yourself to the land and its people, they are all insignificant to me."

"Oh of course, you work for some one else now don't you. What was his name?"

"None of your business. What I do is for me to know only." Karbith turned to face Thalayli.

"You don't even know do you dragon?" Thalayli growled deep from within his chest and glowered at the king.

Karbith then turned to Kaylin, "I will move into the castle in a week from today. That should give you enough time to clear out your belongings. Just because my father thought highly of you does not mean that I do."

Kaylin pulled his gaze from Thalayli and looked at Karbith. "You would throw me out of my home?"

"It is my home now. You have no further use to me or my kingdom. I expect not to see you again."

Kaylin looked shocked, "You are capable of great things Karbith, as was your father, great but terrible. But I want you to know Karbith that you cannot achieve greatness by yourself. To get to the top you will need people to guide you."

"I will achieve greatness on my own, I don't need any one else. Also I intend to finish what my father did not." Karbith's face darkened and it was at this point that Kaylin saw the malice in the boy's eyes.

"Guards!" shouted Kaylin. The guards surrounding Kaylin drew their swords and advanced towards Karbith.

"I will not let you do that Karbith," said Kaylin in a deep, threatening voice. "Your Father was a twisted man. His mind was warped with hatred. The visions he had for this kingdom were terrifying. I can not let you fore fill his plan."

"Is that a challenge, Kaylin?" growled Karbith in reply. The guards continued to approach, surrounding Karbith from all sides.

"Ha, you think you can defeat me, kill me, claim the throne for yourself." Karbith raised his right arm level with his shoulder, a bright white light shone from his palm, and a force seemed to emit from him, causing the guards around him to be thrown high into the air. They landed heavily about twenty feet from where they had stood. They lay sprawled upon the wet ground, their limbs smashed and broken, all of them dead.

Kaylin growled, "You have condemned the entire kingdom to death, all because of blood."

"I care little for blood, I care only for power."

"You can rule a kingdom without having to murder innocent people."

"It is not the humans I wish to dispose of," growled Karbith," that is why I wanted you here Rose. I believe you share my passion for revenge?"

"If you mean the elves?" answered Rose in a questioning tone.
"Yes, I do."

"This is preposterous. There are no such things as elves." Kaylin yelled above the wind that was now beginning to sweep across the marsh land. Rose then turned to face the former king and replied,

"It was only a mere week ago that you believed that dragons did not exist. Yet if my eyes and my mind don't deceive me, and if I may say so that would be extremely unlikely, then there is a dragon stood beside me right this very moment." Kaylin did not answer this; he chose to remain silent, knowing that he was terribly outnumbered, two people and a dragon.

"What is it that you have against the elves?" Rose asked suspiciously, now turning back to Karbith.

"Let's just say, they twisted things that caused me to believe in things that perhaps I would not have believed in if I were in the right frame of mind."

Thalayli, what is going on in Karbith's mind, I know he is using us; but for what. I do not intend to allow myself to be manipulated, again.

I know little of his intentions, I know only as much as you. Remember that revenge is not the answer to everything. To spend your life being eaten away by anger and hate, is not a good life, nor is it a pleasant one. Be wary, yet listen to his plan, we may be able to turn the manipulator into the manipulated.

The girl and the dragon conversed silently whilst Karbith continued to address Kaylin.

"My plan, Kaylin is to recover that which is left of the lord's creation. I must have control of the entire kingdom, all the time the elves live my authority is questionable. I must eradicate the half bloods; the elves and the dwarves. Those who turned from the ways of us humans and raged war upon us so many years ago. They will suffer for what they did, and they will suffer for my father's death."

"It was not elves that killed your father Karbith, you know that. He fell from a ravine. We found his body washed up on the edge of the Orvan River. Karbith you know this, why are you so set on revenge?" Kaylin ventured forwards slightly, however he was still a good ten feet away.

"My father was no simpleton, he was murdered. He was not stupid enough to walk off a cliff, I will find his killer, and I will put them to the same grim fate."

"So that is reason to destroy all these beings that you call elves and dwarves. They have done us no harm Karbith, why can't you see this. Let the past lie dormant, it is no use to us now. It pays us not to bare grudges." Kaylin felt rage begin to bubble inside him, although his lack of courage allowed him to make no further advances, he held his ground. He thought to himself that Karbith's opinion was wrong, what had these secretive people done to the humans of this kingdom. They all lived in peace, they all lived happily; so why should he stand aside and let this monstrous being before him destroy all the peace that he himself had created. After all for the entire period in which Kaylin had been king there had been no trouble; fair enough there had been the slight problem with Rose, but as far as he was aware that was all. Live and let live, he thought to himself.

"Rose, I have heard many things about you. Of course I have heard of the great battle between you and the elves. Even I believe; I was told of your death. Of course how you escaped is not my business, but I believe that perhaps you want revenge on those who made you suffer."

"I care little for the way in which I was treated," She turned briefly to look at Thalayli. "It is the way in which they treated those that I love that gives me the greatest pleasure in making them suffer."

Kaylin felt himself gather courage. He would not stand for this, this destruction of his people. He drew his sword from it sheath; the sound of the blade being drawn caught Karbith's attention. He turned quick as a flash, and he then drew a fine rapier from a sheath at his belt and stood to face Kaylin squarely.

"Are you challenging me, Kaylin? Do you think it wise to cross blades with me?"

"This Karbith is a fight to the death; I will not allow you to fore fill this grotesque dream of yours. Revenge on an innocent race, kill an entire civilization instead of killing the one responsible? You truly are as mad as your father, and you deserve to die, just as he did."

"Are you saying you killed my father?" growled Karbith.

"Ha, no I didn't, but I owe it to the man that did." At this remark Karbith lunged forward. Their blades caught in midair. Their feet moved in a mass of sequences and maneuvers. It seemed that they were one, it was like they were dancing; the dance of death.

Rose sighed and leant against Thalayli. *Typical boys,* She said to the dragon beside her.

If Karbith wishes to kill Kaylin that much why does he not just use magic? Came the dragons reply.

That is a fair point you have made there my friend. Where did Karbith learn magic?

I can only assume that it runs in his blood, after all, his mother could use magic, so perhaps he can too?

Yes, perhaps you are right. But where did he learn it? And also have you not noted his sword? It is an elven blade; the only place he could have got that is from the elves in Elvendin. That's another point, what business does he have with the elves? And why does he not just kill Kaylin, he's just toying with him at the moment.

Rose rolled her eyes; she raised her palm and directed it at the pair of duelers. A ray of black energy shot from her palm and hit Kaylin directly in the chest. The effect was instant; he was dead before he even hit the floor.

"What did you do that for, I was having fun." Retorted the new king.

"To kill some one is one thing, but to make their last few moments here full of pain, fear, and guilt? Now that to me is cruel."

"I gave him a chance to defend himself, just remember he challenged me. I had no intentions of killing him, at this moment in time." He glared at Rose. "Remember who is king now Rose. You are beneath me."

"I am directed by no one, least of all you."

"Are you challenging me as well?"

"No, I am not. You are not worth the effort."

"They sound like the words of a coward." Karbith had hit a nerve, Rose lifted her hand yet again and as she did so Karbith was raised in to the air as if by a noose. He struggled for only a moment before he had fought past her spell and lowered himself back down to the ground.

"Its going to take a lot more than that to over power me Rose." Power seemed to emit from Karbith, his eyes shone with glistening death, a rough wind seemed to envelope him; it then twisted and soared towards Rose. Rose blocked it with a flick of her wrist.

A jet of fire erupted from Karbith's palm and roaring flames flew towards Rose; however it was blocked by a jet of thunderous water.

The pair held this position for a few minutes, each one trying to over come the other.

I will help you. Rose heard Thalayli in her mind and allowed him to merge his energy with hers. As rapidly as the fight had begun, it stopped. The water gushed over Karbith with a force that knocked him fifty feet into the air. The man that had accompanied Karbith came rushing forward from the side of the dirt ridden track to aid his master.

Thanks, said Rose.

Any time, came the reply.

What are we going to do now, he is strong; stronger than we could have expected. Can we stand by and let him take the throne? Rose looked up at the dragon, hoping his reply would answer all of her questions, even those lying deep within her sub-conscience.

Ah, it would seem that perhaps you are beginning to find your path.

Oh shut up with all that crap, else you'll start going on about fate, past lives, memories, souls, heaven and god knows what else. Rose was greatly disappointed by the dragons response; however she pushed the emotion aside as if it had never existed.

The black and red dragon having no clue about the mixed emotions running through Rose seemed to hum with joy.

Rose leapt onto the dragons back and said, *just shh, we have agreed in the past that we must agree to disagree, you think that we all have paths laid out for us when we were made by some creator bloke, and that at the beginning we were all equal, and that in life we have many lessons to learn and that until we learn them all we are reincarnated until we do, then we can pass to a fandabidosie place called utopia, where we will be reunited with our soul mates and live happily ever after. And then of course I believe that when you die you go to a place where everything is nothing, a void, whoopee doo.* The only reply that Rose received was a hearty laugh; and together they took off into the open sky.

. . . .

Dean sat beside Karbith, the king was still breathing, though a few bones appeared broken. Dean remained with Karbith until he began to stir.

"Sire, how are you?"

"Bloody marvelous thanks, you fool of course I'm not ok."

CHAPTER 6

Elvendin

"She thought that she would never be alone, yet when she was lonely she was with the people that should have made her feel the happiest. The only time she was happy was when she had only herself for company. But one day she met someone that truly made her happy; he did not ask her to change, it was total unconditional love. He never left her, they truly were part of each other; they would not have to tell each other how they felt, because they all ready knew. However although they were happy, they lived in fear; fear of loosing each other. Then the day came when she died. He said he would never leave her, yet when she closed her eyes for the last time and saw nothing, he was no longer there; and she was alone."

Nenamis and Laylan were walking through a rich green forest. The trees here seemed to radiate there own light, like they were producing an energy of their own and it was seeping out through its bark. The woods canopy was over a hundred feet high, and rays of light shone down through the leaves casting rays of light that appeared to come from heaven itself; as though the angels were attempting to share with the world below, their joyous heavenly world up above. Sarabie enjoyed the scenery from the safety of Nenamis's back; she took in every scent, every sight and every sound.

Bird song followed the trio through the forest, however no other sound was heard. For the majority of the first half of the day they walked in silence as Sarabie tried to reserve her strength. However after realizing that it took little effort to talk to Nenamis, she spent the morning deep in conversation.

Where did your egg come from?

My egg was stolen from your mother by your father. I was given to your mother by the elves. The elves were given my egg by the earth.

How did my mother know the elves; and how did the elves get your egg, did they find it somewhere? Sarabie was overwhelmed with questions, however she understood that perhaps spilling them all at once was not the wisest of plans; therefore she reserved herself to three of her fifty questions.

No you miss understand me. They were given it. You will understand once you have met them. As for the other question you asked, I do not know what your mother has to do with the elves; all the time I was an egg I could sense the presence of people, yet I could not see or hear them. It was for this reason that I hatched for you as soon as you laid your hands upon the surface of my egg. I could sense it was you, I could sense that you were the one.

Sarabie gazed down at the back of Nenamis's head. As he walked he snaked his grand head around to look at her. The girl smiled at the dragon; Nenamis then swung his head around to see where he was going before he ended up walking into something.

But I want to know everything now. There is so much I don't know. Sarabie once again resolved herself to her curiosity.

Well the elves are incredibly peaceful beings. They live with the forest. They create their homes from the trees branches. Their existence has no effect on the environment. They were sent to this earth by the great lord above, their reason for being here was to guard the earth, and to help the other beings on their paths to heaven. However they were treated badly, following this they went in to hiding hoping that one day some one would help them show the beings of the world how to live their lives, and live them to the maximum. The lord felt betrayed by the elves and offered them no help; the great creator could not find with in himself the forgiveness required to aid the elves when they needed their lord the most. He sent down upon the earth us dragons. We also, were defeated, but amongst my people a prophecy was told; a prophecy of a girl and a dragon.

There was a silence held between them for a while as Sarabie pondered this thought. She wondered if this prophecy of a girl and a dragon could possibly have anything to do with Nenamis and herself.

What did the prophecy say?

When every thing we have is lost
And the light seems non-existent
Look down below the crust of the earth
And there you shall find your hope

Upon its back between its tines
Shall sit a girl of power
Her power shall match that of the lord
For her soul will be merged forever

Her souls other half will have hide of red
Yet he shall be marked by a dark power
Which he shall no of not
Only she will have the answer

Our saviors they will be
Though she will have a choice
Evil will persuade her
And hell may be her path

A scar will wrench her soul
And blacken it like coal
For she may meet an equal
And be darkened to his ways

Between the good and evil
There lies the thinnest line
Then sacrifice will be made
And what's left shall linger forever

So when the Sheppard's warning has meaning
Look up to the skies
There a dragon shall be soaring high
With flame upon is tongue

Magic will be her power
Magic will be her might
Magic will be her evil
Magic will be her choice

Nenamis's words hung in Sarabie's conscience; they seemed to haunt her very being.

And you think this has something to do with us?

Well yes they do.

But I don't have a scar or a power or anything really, I'm just me. Sarabie sunk in to herself and feared that perhaps all of this was a mistake, and a fear crept forward, that once the elves realized their mistake they would sent her back to the castle, and her Father.

Well, just me; If it is not about us then perhaps someone in the future may hold the answer, but for now we must train hard so that perhaps when the time comes, we can help the chosen ones.

"We are not far now Sarabie," said Laylan from just in front of them; his voice deep yet relaxed. However Sarabie ignored Laylan and continued to converse with Nenamis; already it was apparent to the dragon and the elf that the young girl had a distinct disregard for authority, as she continually ignored any instruction directed at her, as they made their way towards Elvendin. However Sarabie noted that her surroundings had changed an incredibly small amount and that, therefore, was the reason for her deciding that they still had a little while longer before they arrived at their destination; hence, she choice not to answer Laylan. She also felt that her conversation with Nenamis was far more important than anything the elf had to say.

Are you marked by a dark power? Sarabie asked Nenamis tentatively now fearing that he had some deep dark vicious side that she would, personally, not like to cross.

Not that I am aware of, however I am still young. We must wait and see what the future brings. May I ask the nature of your past? I have, it would seem, rescued you from a most horrid fate, as has Laylan. Nenamis was hesitant in asking Sarabie about her past in case it caused her to loose faith in him as a friend, or perhaps she became enraged with bitterness towards her Father. However Sarabie answered quietly and calmly; and in her conscience, Nenamis could feel the acceptance of her past.

I was four when my brother was born. Sarabie began hesitantly, unaware of how to begin a subject in which she found incredibly difficult to discuss as she had never, in the past, talked to any one about her thoughts or feelings. After all, never before in her life had any one cared enough for her to ask her how she felt. *His name was Karbith. I was hated by my father from the day I was born. My fathers name was Gaston, he*

longed for power, and he seemed to think that he was better than everyone else. He
wanted to dispose of all those people that he deemed unworthy of life.

When my mother fell pregnant with me, my father hoped that I would be a boy.
His opinion was that women were beneath men, he wanted a family of boys, and he
prayed that his eldest would become king not queen. Of course by the ancient rules
laid down by our people, the eldest child takes the throne when their parents die
whether they are male or female. So of course when I was born, my father felt that
my mother had failed him. He beat her within an inch of her life; she had many
scars from by father that stayed with her right up until the day she died.

I am sorry I could not have saved your mother as well as you.

That's ok Nenamis. It wasn't your fault, I guess she was just meant to go;
maybe she is happier where she is now. Sarabie hung her head, and Nenamis
felt the sadness in her heart that stemmed from her feeling of longing,
longing to be normal and have a normal family that loved her. It was
apparent to the great dragon that that was all that the young girl wanted,
was to be loved.

Anyway, she fell pregnant a while after, this time it was a boy. My father was
most pleased. However he still had to solve the problem that I was the first born;
my father intended to stage my death, yet my mother protected me. She begged him
not to kill me. He chose to lock me away instead and tell everyone that I was dead.
I remember my mother's screams as my father abused her. I saw a lot of it before
I was locked away. As I said before my father had no mercy; it was as though he
was completely unable to feel compassion towards another being. My mother had the
most horrid scar on her leg from his blade, from when he had lost his temper one
night. Every time I saw my mother she had a fresh bout of cuts and bruises. After
five years of this, the beatings stopped. I do not know why, my mother visited me
more often, almost every day. Occasionally Gaston would come and beat me. All I
wanted in the end was to lie down and not get up; for everything to be over, I just
wanted to die. I saw no reason to live. I could not foresee a better life for myself. I
saw little day light, and spoke to no one. I just didn't want to be alone. I felt that if
I died no one would care. I had nothing to fight for, just an empty, hollow existence.
I wished sometimes that I would just die, stop breathing, sometimes I felt so close
to death. I longed every day for death to take me; I begged, yet each day passed and
my pain just grew. It felt as though even death hated me and that some one out there
wanted me to suffer like this, as though I was meant to feel this amount of pain.
I didn't understand how the world could treat me like this, why everyone else was
loved and cared for, how everyone else had a family; yet I did not. It just didn't seem
fair. There were times I wondered if perhaps there were people out there who were

suffering worse than me, and if maybe I was being weak and just feeling sorry for myself. It was times like these that I tried to pull myself together and be strong if not for myself but for the other people out there who were also struggling through life. But then through lack of strength I would just fall back in to a dark whole deep inside myself and continue struggling in my black abyss of sorrow. Back then, there was nothing for me, no one. Sarabie paused as tears slowly trickled down her face and dripped heavily on to the dragons scaled back. Through all the years in which Sarabie had sat alone in her cell, not once had she shed a tear, yet now she knew that some one cared it seemed to her that the tears would never stop. *Nenamis, what happened to my father?*

He lived.

I wish he hadn't, he deserved to die.

No, Sarabie, it is not up to us to judge the length of a person's life. Do not be so hasty to judge some one; however they have treated you or those around you.

Sarabie did not answer the dragon, she remained deep in thought.

"We are here." Sarabie looked at Laylan, still registering what he had said. She looked at the elf and felt an admiration for him, stood there so bold and confident; he seemed completely at peace with his surroundings, as though this was exactly where he was meant to be.

"Sarabie?" she came out of her daydream and looked around; Laylan's voice was so soft and understanding, it seemed to wash away all off Sarabie's trouble, and make things appear effortless. The forest surrounding them appeared the same, the trees tall, the forest canopy allowing rays of light to fall upon the leaf covered ground.

"What do you mean we are here, I don't see anything different?" Sarabie took in the forest about her, straining her eyes trying to find something that she thought perhaps wasn't really there.

"Look harder." Sarabie looked around the wood again. As she examined her surroundings she noticed tracks leading in and out of the trees. Upon the trees bark were ridges that resembled steps, they led up to dense patches of leaves. The leaves and branches formed small houses right in the tops of the trees. She gazed at the surprisingly beautiful civilization around her. From behind trees, and from deep within their branches appeared the most fantastic beings Sarabie had ever seen; their faces were elegant, they moved with a superior grace, their ears were pointed and their hair silky and well kept. The faces of the elves held an immense beauty in which Sarabie had never seen before; it seemed to her that although they fitted in perfectly with their surroundings, they had in fact come from another realm, a place most heavenly and wonderful. This therefore caused the young girl to wonder if there was more to these people than met the eye. Perhaps they were more superior to the other humans in which she had met. However this then led her to realize that the only folk she had met in her life was her mother and father, so therefore she then felt that perhaps she did not have the right to make a negative comparison between the humans and the elves. However it was clear to Sarabie that the elves were indeed the most beautiful people she had ever seen.

"Welcome to Elvendin." Elves were now approaching from all directions and had soon surrounded Sarabie and Nenamis. The beings seemed to swarm around the pair; each person wanting a glimpse of the dragon and his rider. Many of the splendid elves bowed to Sarabie and Nenamis, some greeted them heartily and others reached out trying to shake Sarabie's hand and touch Nenamis's bright, gem like scales.

From within the crowd approached a tall woman with long brown hair that reached the small of her back. Her eyes were the same color as her hair and she was light and slender. She appeared to be putting little effort into her movement, and just seemed to float over the ground. Her face was sharp and angular, much like that of a cat; and the elf just seemed so graceful, as though the earth did not even shift under her footfall.

"Greetings Sarabie, my name is Carman. You have been long awaited amongst my people. You are a gift to us and are our only ray of hope." Her voice was smooth and silky, almost as though she was singing. Sarabie bowed slightly, "This is Niver Nenamis, Nenamis for short," said Sarabie. Carman turned to face the dragon and bowed incredibly low, and said "I am pleased to meet you, Niver Nenamis."

It is a pleasure to meet you too, Carman. Carman heard this in her conscious and nodded an acknowledgement. She turned to face Laylan, "Will you escort Sarabie and Nenamis to their new home please, and explain to them what will happen and discuss the training in which they will receive."

Laylan nodded, "Sarabie, Nenamis will you follow me please."

"I will see you in the morning." Carman smiled and turned to address the crowd, "everyone, please do not disturb Nenamis or Sarabie tonight. Let them rest, when they have gathered strength then we will celebrate with a grand feast." The crowd dispersed leaving only

Laylan. He strode forward down a path that led even deeper into the forest. They walked for only a few minutes before Laylan stopped and looked up at a large, old, oak tree. The elf pointed at some ridges in the tree trunk, "These are the steps you should use to get to the tree house. It is large enough for Nenamis," He looked at the dragon, "You must fly just below the forest canopy and enter a gap in the wall of leaves. You should find your accommodation satisfactory, however if you have any problems just give me a shout, I live in a tree a few yards further down the track. Now tomorrow I will come and get you and around eight o'clock. I will then take you to Carman, she will either instruct you herself, or allocate you a tutor. You will study elvish, magic, archery and swordsmanship. Also you will learn how to control your mind. Nenamis, you will learn with Sarabie, this is so that you can aid her when she is lost. After all two minds are better than one. Remember you are our hope; there is a tremendous weight on both your shoulders. Please try your hardest to do us proud.

Now I will leave you to a-customize yourself to your new home. I will send someone up to serve you dinner later on this evening; I will also send breakfast for you at around seven o'clock in the morning." Laylan paused, looking at Sarabie, "I will also have some fresh clothes sent up for you."

"Thank you," said Sarabie.

"Good night, I shall see you tomorrow."

"Yes, see you in the morning. Thank you for all the help you have given me."

Laylan nodded and turned to follow the track further into the forest.

. . . .

Sarabie climbed the steps into the tree house. When she reached the top she found an entrance consisting of heavily intertwined vines. She pushed them to one side and made her way into a large circular room. From the inside you would never have thought that you were living in a tree. The walls were draped with light blue cloth, and in the centre of the room was a hollow that was lined also with light blue cloth. To one side of the hollow was a circular bed. It was made from branches that had twisted around each other to form a base. Upon the branches was a thick woolen cloth. The bed was then dressed with blue silk covers and pillows. At the back of the circular room was a wide entrance that was similar to the one Sarabie had entered through except that it was about ten times the size. Next to the entrance was a long rope. Sarabie, full of curiosity, pulled the rope. The vine curtains were then drawn back to reveal a balcony on which sat Nenamis.

About bloody time, I thought you were never going to let me in.

Sorry, its just, well, it's amazing. All my life I have been treated as though I was worthless. Now people are saying that I am their only hope. I'm going to learn so much. My life is changing, for the better. I have a purpose; I am a ray of hope for others. I just want to put the world right, and prevent other people suffering as I did.

Mmm.

. . . .

"Good evening Laylan."

"Good evening Carman, you asked to see me?" Laylan was in a small clearing full of snowdrops. The small drops of heaven glistened white in the soft moonlight that shone through the tree tops. They seemed to cover the forest floor like a carpet; a beautiful sea of miniature silver stars, right beneath the very feet of those who walked upon them. Even those who did not appreciate the beauty of the world noticed the most fantastic presence of these most brilliant flowers. It was often wondered by some, how it was possible for these small glistening white flowers to stir so many emotions within a person; it felt sometimes as though the snowdrops were reaching right in to the very soul and raising each dark emotion from deep within and bringing it to the surface where it can finally be dealt with and put aside, allowing the person to finally move on and see life for what it really is. Therefore it appeared, to many, that the snowdrops allowed people to see things more clearly and understand things that had before seemed completely uncomprehendable. This was perhaps why the elves chose this particular clearing to sit and ponder upon their troubles and woes; they also chose this particular part of the great forest of Elvendin, to hold their woodland gatherings where in which they would discuss any issues in which they had with in their peaceful lives.

This consequently was the reason why Carman had chosen this spot to speak with Laylan. The slender female elf was sat on a small boulder that seemed to serve well as a bench; she motioned for Laylan to join her.

"I see you have faired well considering the nature of your trip."

"Yes well, Nenamis brought Sarabie to me, I was not needed."

"Were there any wounds to heal?"

"Yes, two major wounds and bruising on her neck. I healed all of them. However she has received emotional pain, of course no one can heal that but Sarabie."

"Yes, I agree. We must keep a close eye on her. After all the prophecy says she may loose faith and turn against us. I just hope that circumstances do not allow this."

"I do not think she has a bad heart. She will do her best to become what we want her to be. My fear however is that it becomes so that it is not her choice. After all she is a living soul, just like the rest of us, does she really deserve the fate that awaits her?" Laylan peered intently in to Carman's eyes hoping that her reply would answer all of his uncertainties.

"No one deserves that fate, however Sarabie is different. She has been given to us to for fill the prophecy. She has a job to do. At the end of the day, her soul is worth the sacrifice if millions can then live in harmony."

Laylan did not answer; he remained in silence, admiring the beauty of his surroundings. He wondered if, should the war be fought, whether he would ever see this beauty again.

"Laylan, I wish for you to train Sarabie. She knows you; after all you are the first elf she believes to have met. Also I believe that you are one of the few that know Sarabie's complete history; and future"

Laylan thought momentarily. "I will be glad to have the honor of training our savior."

"I want you to gain her trust. Get her to tell you everything. She will confide in the dragon, but I wish for her to confide in you as well. Then I want you to return to me and tell me everything she has told you; when the time comes, it will be vital for us to know everything, all of her weaknesses and all of her strengths. Is that understood?"

"No. I will not do that." Laylan looked aghast and stared bitterly at Carman.

"And why not?"

"That is a breach of her confidence, and I don't wish for you to think of her as something in which you can control."

"I want you to realize something Laylan, It is by our doing that she has that dragon. If it were not for us and her mother, she would not have been born."

"She did not ask for this to happen to her."

"No, she did not. The lord did. You must do as you are ordered Laylan; I think you need to remember that you made a choice long ago. You chose to be in this position."

Laylan remained silent for a while, deep in thought.

"Yes Carman, I forgot my place. I will report back to you every evening after Sarabie's training. Good night." With that Laylan rose and walked out of the clearing, back in the direction of his home.

"Good night Laylan."

CHAPTER 7

Jack's hope

*"You can only go so far in life, before you realize that
something's missing. The only question is what?"*

JACK WAS SAT on the Eastern shore of Harbia; his feet were resting
in the water. The tide washed in and out, clawing at the sand that
lay resting upon the beach. Tears rolled down his face and onto his
tunic. His blonde fringe fell across his face; the rest of his hair was
blowing softly in the wind. He shivered slightly in the cold, however he
continued to sit there on the beach, alone and unmoving.

*Why do I feel like this? I hate him, why has he left me. Am I really not good
enough for him? I always wanted to be like him when I was younger, I respected
him, and I even wanted to be like him. Grr why is he such an asshole? He deserves
do die, he should die. Why is Karbith so much better than me? What does he have
that I don't? Well I suppose he is clever, he has power, he is handsome and he can
offer more to Dean than I can. Maybe he is better of without me. I don't think I
can do this any more.*

Jack thought to himself as he sat there alone; his body shuddered
as he slowly broke down in to a mad burst of rage and hate, along with
a bitter sadness that ate away at his soul.

"Lord! Why do you hate me so much? Why have you and my
brother abandoned me? I need him? I need some one. I can't be alone.

I can't do it, life is too hard to battle on you're own. I need him, I need
him?" Jack's voice slowly broke into a coarse whisper, as his voice box
complained at the volume of his raging shouts. "I can't do this any
more. There is nothing for me here. There is no point to my existence.
I should just give up and not live any more." Tears ran steadily down
his face and slowly they dried causing his skin to feel dry and slightly
crispy. Yet he did not make any motion to wipe away the frozen tears.

"The world would be a better place with out me? I'm a waste of
space; my meager existence is pathetically worthless. I am no good to
anyone. I have ruined Dean's life, he really is better off without me."
Jack had a gaping hole in his heart that he felt could never be filled
again. To him Dean really was part of him and he had always believed
that they would be together forever. Now, do not get me wrong when
I say that Jack loved Dean, for he did however not in the same way
that perhaps a husband loves his wife. Yet the principle still remains
that Jacks love and adoration for Dean was real and true, and it was
mentally impossible for Jack to live with out Dean. After all Jack had
given Dean his soul, and we all know that with out a soul in return, life
truly does become impossible; because for one person to love another,
yet not to have that person share the same love for you, really does
tear a person apart; and quite rapidly life is destroyed, and nothing
seems real anymore except for the pain deep inside your soul, and the
constant shredding of you're heart every day that you're alone.

"I can't live anymore. Maybe Dean really is better off without me."

Do you really think that? Jack heard a voice deep from within his
mind.

What! Who are you?

I am someone who can help you.

Why would any one want to help me? Jack's body gave another unexpected
shudder, as he struggled to keep his breath steady.

I want to help you because that is what I do.

Are you an angel?

Of sort.

So you will help me, how?

*Do you seek revenge? After all you did not deserve to be treated the way you
were. You are equal to everyone else. Why should you be made to suffer and not
him. You loved him, you cared for him for twenty five years, yet he took it all for*

granted, he threw it aside with no consideration. He didn't help you, he never cared for you, and he never loved you, not like you loved him.

Jack slowly could feel anger welling up inside him; ready to burst. *How can you help me?*

I can give you a power; a power to destroy the one who made you suffer.

What must I do?

I ask very little.

What?

I will grant you this power, with it you can do what you wish; however in time I may come to ask you a favor. You must use your power to for fill what is asked of you.

Yes, I will do it. Jack answered in hast, his anger eating away at his soul until he had no other emotions left.

You must sign a contract, well a blood pact really.

What do I have to do?

Before you is a black stone, it is called onyx. Upon it you must leave a trace of your blood. The stone will absorb the blood, following this my blood will begin to ooze from the stone, tip the blood from the stone into your cut, this will transfer the power I have promised to you.

Now, had this particular offer been made to a person who perhaps had not endured much emotional trauma, then they would of course thought to themselves that blood does not ooze from stones, and one should not be hearing voices in their head. So therefore it could easily have be said that a blood pact such as this would not be done by some one in their right mind, and therefore it is questionable as to the true nature of the deal.

Yet disregarding all logic, Jack withdrew a dagger from his belt; he sliced the palm of his hand and held the stone tightly within it. After a minute or two Jack placed the stone in his other hand and watched as the blood was absorbed into the stone. Immediately a black substance seeped from the stones surface. Jack assumed that this was the blood and placed it back into his bleeding hand. As soon as the black blood and the red blood merged, Jack felt strength enter him. His mind suddenly boggled with thoughts, he could hear a voice on the wind, he could hear all the beings around him, sensed them, heard their thoughts. He raised his hand and directed it at a stone on the ground. Slowly the stone began to rise, he applied more force to his action and the stone flew into the air and landed over a hundred feet away in the sea.

Jack went to talk to the person in his head but found that he had gone. Fully aware of his surroundings, Jack leapt up and back flipped onto the grass. He felt his muscles surge with power, felt every cell in his body, however emotionally he felt only anger.

Jack felt that he was now invincible and that no harm could ever come to him again. However he failed to realize that his soul was still not complete, and his heart was still torn. Yet now he felt only bitterness and anger; his urge for revenge had shunted out the sadness and loneliness. Jack could now feel nothing emotional wise. He had been hurt so much by his brother that he could feel no more; it was as though that part of him no longer existed. Jack knew this, yet he believed that this made him stronger, if he could not feel, then he could not be hurt. He had no intention of ever suffering again.

And so it was with his new found power, Jack grinned to himself and whispered, "I will have my revenge."

CHAPTER 8

Dean's Army

"There are times in our lives when we can do the right thing, though
we may have to put ourselves out. However at what cost to others
would it be if we chose to ignore these moments?"

DEAN WAS WAITING in the courtyard outside the castle; it was raining lightly, the sky a murky grey. It appeared to an onlooker that perhaps the sky was mimicking the mood that was being felt in the courtyard below. Dean paced nervously up and down the yard, waiting for his master. Had he had to wait for a longer period of time than necessary then it could have been possible for him to wear away at the ancient cobbles beneath his feet. However lucky for the cobbles Dean was not to pace for long.

The bold young man felt nervous yet excited, happy and sad, angry and frustrated. His legs beginning to ache, he sat down on a small wall surrounding a fountain, the same fountain in which Kaylin had sat previously in his reign as king. His legs trembled in the cold, or perhaps it was nerves of his masters anticipated instructions.

Dean heard footsteps behind him, stood up and spun around. Before him stood Karbith, now he wore rich magenta robes and walked with a new authority.

"Good morning Dean." Karbith inclined his head politely; however he felt no respect towards the man before him.

"Good morning your majesty," Dean bowed low, and avoided looking directly at Karbith.

"I trust that you are aware of the following proceedings?"

"I am afraid not fully sire." Dean shook his head and continued to admire his shoes which were a muddy brown due to the increasing amount of dirt in which was gathering upon them from his pacing upon the murky cobbles, and now of course the true color of his shoes was now completely unknown.

"I chose you over your brother because of your brains, perhaps I was wrong. However, this time I shall let it slip. I want you to raid all the villages and towns in the kingdom. From these towns you will take all men between the age of sixteen and forty and create an army. You must train this army to the highest possible standard. I will give your army protection using magic. Once you have gathered an army of great force you shall return here, to me. I give you six weeks to complete your task. Following this you must hunt down the elves and the dwarves, they must be destroyed. As for Rose, I will make it my personal mission to put an end to her, and that dragon. Are there any questions you would like to ask?"

"How will I find the dwarves and the elves?" Dean asked tentatively.

"I will tell you when the time comes, fortune may even shine upon us and they seek us."

"How will I persuade the men join my army?"

"I have already recruited some young men for the army, they have been fully trained and prepped; they will aid you in your quest. Should any men refuse to join, threaten their families, if all else fails, kill the ones they love. Just remember Dean, there is no better form of motivation than revenge. Now go; there are four hundred men outside the castle grounds waiting for your command. I suggest you leave tonight. Now good day to you; have a good trip." Karbith nodded, turned, and strode back into the castle through the huge oaken doors that seemed to tower over the court yard, leaving Dean standing alone with only the rain for company. It now appeared to Dean that the courtyard and the castle grounds were a form of safe hold for him; it was as though the entire time in which he was this side of the castle walls he was safe and could come to no harm. It was like the rest of the world failed to exist, and as if what had transpired between him and jack had not really happened. That was currently how Dean was coping with what he had done; he was trying to pretend that Jack did not exist. Now however Dean had to leave the castle and face reality; it was now that Dean had to deal with what he had done. Dean knew that they way in which he had treated Jack was wrong, and now he regretted it. But it was too late to put things right.

. . . .

Dean turned to look at the castle one last time, he felt alone. He then turned to face the army of men awaiting him. They all sat astride mighty war horses, big, bold animals that jostled in the rain. Dean strode up to a grey mare that was saddled and waiting for him. He gracefully pulled himself on to her back and asked the mare to face the other horses. He felt a sudden thrill as he sat astride the horse, their energy seemed to merge so that they became one; he only had to think of his command for her and she would for fill it. However even though the mare trusted Dean she still felt unsettled beneath him for she could sense the tension in the air.

"Men, I am your commander, you will address me as sir. Any orders I give you must be followed, else your life will be forfeit. We leave now for Teridin. The population there is seven hundred; there should be around three hundred men, this will almost double our numbers already. You must share with your comrades your knowledge and experience. As our numbers grow so will our skill. We will rid this kingdom of filth, we will make this kingdom pure, we will rid this kingdom of those who turned on us in the past, and we will make this kingdom truly our own. Now we will ride upon our steeds, we will entrust them with our lives, trust them and they will trust us, it is then that they will carry us in to the midst of a battle. Now let's ride!" Dean spurred his horse into a trot, the other men and their steeds followed, some of the horses bursting into canter with the excitement. And together the small army made their way away from the castle and within no time, their forms were hidden by the rains mist.

CHAPTER 9

An Unheeded Warning

*"Fly away from your troubles
Run away from your sorrows
Sour across the open waves
And disappear to a land that is safe
Go where only you can go
And don't let anyone in
Your mind is your own
For only you to see
So make it what you want
And with it you can do as you please"*

ROSE WANDERED THE forest alone. Thalayli was nearby, however due to his size he found it very difficult to fit beneath the trees canopy. She walked with an elegant grace, being part elf, she appeared incredibly graceful. Her ears were pointed only slightly, however everything else about her fully resembled that of an elf. She bothered little about her appearance; she wore brown leather boots that came mid way up her calf, she wore brown calf skin leggings that were tucked into her boots, and her bodice also was made of brown calf skin that was laced up at the back. Currently her hair was tied back by a small strip of leather.

Rose stopped and stood perfectly still. She heard something on the breeze, a whisper, someone was approaching. Gracefully she leapt in to the nearest tree; Rose being stronger than any normal being, was able to jump twenty feet into the air with ease just in time as a man walked around the corner.

He had short, scruffy brown hair; his fringe fell with a casual elegance across his face. He had prominently pointed ears. He walked with grace, and seemed to be at one with the world around him.

"Laylan!" Rose jumped from the tree and landed before Laylan. She left barely a mark upon the earth as she landed so lightly considering the height in which she had dropped from.

"Rose now isn't it?"

"Yes." Laylan smiled and sat beside a birch tree. Rose sat crossed legged opposite him. They settled within each others company.

"Last time I heard, you were dead."

"You know it's funny, I met up with a couple of old friends the other day and they said exactly the same."

"Ye, that is rather funny really, I wonder why every one would go round thinking you were dead?"

"Haven't got the foggiest idea," Rose laughed and grinned at the elf.

"I guess you're not intending to tell me what happened?"

"Even if I told you what happened; I don't think you would believe me."

"Try me." Rose hesitated.

"I don't really think that I am in the mood for reciting old wrongs."

"Why did you come looking for me Rose?"

"Why did you come looking for me?"

"I heard you were up to your old tricks, so I wanted to know what you were up to, after all I heard very little of you for such a long time, and I hate to say it but; I missed you. When I heard you were still alive I just had to come and see you. People were talking Rose, saying that you were killed by my people, that you spend time in the black abyss between heaven and hell; that you were thrown in to hell, and that you were so evil that the devil himself threw you back out. Is any of it true?"

"Bollocks is it, are you really stupid enough to believe everything that you hear?"

"You really think I would believe it all? No, I do not. However there are elements of it that are quite contemplate-able." Laylan picked up a white snowdrop that was quivering beside him. He drew his hand over it and the flower seemed to emit a white glow.

"So which part do you believe, the part where I was lost in the void, or the part where I was thrown out of hell?" Rose said this calmly, however there was a note of sarcasm in her voice.

"It does not matter what I believe, what only matters is the truth."

"You are of the same opinion as Thalayli when it comes to the truth."

"Is that such a bad thing that we should both chose to follow the path that is most obvious and is most clearly acceptable?"

"You understand my opinion on this matter."

"Yes I do, but that is what I find most frustrating; you see you are unable to see things from another person's perspective, once upon a time this was your greatest gift, now however it is your biggest weakness." Rose remained silent; she chose to examine the ground beneath which she was sat.

"You cannot deny it Rose, death has changed you,"

"Are you saying that if you died, were thrown in to hell and shown many things that you never thought possible, that you could return to the earth unscathed, unharmed emotionally?"

"I did not say that."

"It is what you implied."

"I am sorry if it offended you, however I feel that emotion escaped you a long time ago, even perhaps, before you died."

"I have no need for emotions any more; I have felt too much pain to know that emotions only bring a deeper darker hell right in your very soul."

"I have known you for a long time Rose; I understand the pain you have felt."

"You are wrong, you have no idea how I felt."

"Perhaps," Laylan placed the snowdrop back upon its stalk. Still glowing the two parts of the plant merged together, forming an entirely new plant. The flowers began to glow silver and were larger than before. The stem turned gold and glistened in the sunlight; it radiated an energy of its own, seemingly filling the entire glen with a new peaceful beauty.

Rose gazed upon the flower longingly, "I have been unable to do that for a long time; I fear I have lost the skill."

Laylan laughed, "Rose you are wise enough now to know that it takes little skill to create what I have just created, it takes love, and it is that very emotion that you seem to lack the most."

"All of those that I loved have died, therefore my love died with them."

"What about Thalayli, do you not love him?" Rose turned away from Laylan and did not answer him.

"You fear to love him in case he is also taken from you." Still Rose did not answer.

"Why were you looking for me?" Laylan saw a flicker of sadness behind Rose's eyes so chose to change the subject for he fancied not having his neck broken.

"I have come to warn you."

"Me?"

"Yes, well the elves really. Karbith has claimed the throne; he intends to destroy your race and that of the dwarves."

"I am afraid that I have been, shall we say, removed from Elvendin; I am unable to return. Therefore I will not be able to relay your message." The pair sat in silence for a while, both of them deep in thought.

"It would then seem that neither races, dwarves nor elves, will be warned of the upcoming events," commented Laylan.

"So it would seem."

"Yes so it would seem."

Rose found this comment frustrating and did not hesitate to retort, "You think that I should walk openly in to Elvendin and deliver them a warning message of war and expect them to believe me and then walk out alive? Some how I doubt awfully that would work."

"And what about the dwarves?"

"They would not hesitate to kill me either."

"Perhaps it is all you deserve after what you did to them." Rose chose, once again, to look in the other direction and avoid answering the question.

"Perhaps we could warn them together, after all, we are both unwelcomed by both race's, and I personally would rather warn them and them take no notice of my words, than not warn them at all. Also I do rather like saying I told you so."

Rose smiled and replied, "It would be just like the old times."

"Yes, I feel that I am quite in the mood for an adventure, after all trouble seems to follow you around where ever you go."

"Are you saying that I cause trouble, or that trouble is caused because I am merely present?"

"Both, now where is Thalayli? I haven't seen him for far too many years,"

"He cannot enter the forest, he is to big now."

"Bloody hell, well shall we get going." Laylan got to his feet and offered Rose his hand; Rose looked up in to his face, deep in thought seemingly as though a great decision was being made just by taking his hand. She took it and gracefully got to her feet.

"To Elvendin then;" and with that the elf and the part blood strode into the forest.

. . . .

Thalayli waited on the outskirts of the forest; he called out to Rose with his mind but received no answer. He remained in the same spot for hours, listening, watching.

He heard them before he saw them. Thalayli felt Rose's mind and began to probe her for answers.

He is with you, what did he say?

We are going to Elvendin, we intend to warn them.

And the dwarves?

I do not know, there is a chance that once we enter Elvendin, we may not leave.

Laylan and Rose strode from within the depths of the forest. The two beings appeared majestically striding towards Thalayli, side by side; each of them having their own immense beauty and a most powerful energy that seemed to over power all of the other energy around them until the only noticeable beings left were themselves.

Laylan bowed low and greeted Thalayli. "It has been a long while, too long I fear."

It has been a while; perhaps your presence will be appreciated.

Laylan answered the dragon with his mind, *Rose has changed, and not for the better.*

Yes I agree, we have drifted apart, I fear our bond is weakening.

Before, I could sense your presence within her, now however it is as though you are not even there.

The dragon hung his head low and a deep rumbling came from deep from within his chest.

I fear for the worst, Laylan.

The elf nodded solemnly and turned to face Rose. "Shall we go then?"

"Yes let's get this over and done with. We shall ride there." The elf and the part blood climbed upon the dragon, and then Thalayli leapt in to the air with one mighty leap. He beat the air with his powerful wings; he was completely at one with the sky, soaring through with the wind.

After a couple of hours, the beating rhythm of Thalayli's wings began to slow, he tipped forward in the air and prepared to land. The mighty dragon sped towards the ground like a speeding bullet, as the earth rapidly drew closer, he did not slow. Then when he was only about twenty feet from the Earth he spread his wings to their maximum length and arched his body to absorb the impact of his landing.

The ground shook beneath the powerful dragon, the tree's swayed silently in the breeze and the sun shone brightly down upon them. Rose and Laylan leapt from the dragon and landed silently upon the grass beside him.

"You both remember the way I trust?" asked Laylan.

"How could I forget?" Rose strode into the forest, followed by the dragon and the elf. The forest of Elvendin was far larger than any of the other forests of Garathien; the trees stood taller and further apart, and the forest floor was brighter as more light was able to pass through the forest canopy than in any other forest.

They walked for half an hour before they reached a small clearing, houses were concealed deep within the tree's branches, and small tracks led deeper into the forest. At the bottom of the high old oak tree's were small collections of white snowdrops; every thing about the clearing was peaceful; it was easy to completely forget about the outside world. It was this small paradise that had kept the elves happy as they hid away from the rest of the world; this enchanting place caused them to believe that their existence was perfect and that nothing could ever go wrong.

However Rose and Laylan felt anything but at peace, within seconds of them entering the clearing, they saw elves appear from every tree visible, they were all armed with bows and arrows and they were all directed at Rose. She did not flinch, or at all look surprised to have her life threatened in this manner. Rose rolled her eyes and turned to face the woman walking towards them.

"How dare you enter Elvendin? You are neither human nor elf, you don't even have a soul; you don't belong in this world. You are not welcome."

"I guessed that when I found fifty arrows aimed at my head. I have come to warn you Carman."

"I have no time for your games; you are not whole, you are evil and should not filth Elvendin with your presence. You will not leave now though, instead you must die; I will not have you destroy my home. Seize her!" Fifty jets of light hit her at once, Rose crumbled to the ground, only being able to block half of the spells. She lay unconscious on the ground as vines crept along the floor and wound themselves tightly around her body. Thalayli roared and sent jets of black fire soaring around the glen. The elves shot hundreds of flaming arrows towards the dragon. He bellowed again as yet another course of arrows came his way.

"Stop this" yelled Laylan. He was ignored and the dragon's strength began to fail. Blood spurted from his body; an arrows protruding from his left eye. Thalayli let out a soul piercing scream, the elves, for a split second, hesitated; they then proceeded to shower him in spells that paralyzed him. He let out a final scream and collapsed; the vines then winding themselves around his body just as they had done with Rose.

"What have you done?" screamed Laylan.

"What we said we would, should she return. As for you Laylan, you too were banished; why have you returned?"

"To warn you Carman, Karbith has claimed the throne of men; he intends to destroy our entire race and that of the dwarves."

"And why should I believe you, it would not be the first time that you have lied to us all Laylan? Remember, you said that she was dead!" Carman glared harshly at Laylan, "Then do please remember that you chose your position, you chose to be banished. It was your choice to become an outcast, so why have you returned, to trick us all perhaps?"

"I am not lying to you, I speak only the truth. He is gathering an army; he will strike in a matter of weeks. You must prepare to fight."

"Since when were you the leader of the elves?" Laylan dropped his head and gazed at the floor.

"I am not instructing you on what to do, I am merely advising you."

"You are in no position to offer me advice; I fear you forget your place."

"So you will not fight Karbith?"

"No, I will not bring war upon the kingdom, Elvendin is a peaceful place, I will not allow for my people to fight for a false cause."

Laylan felt broken, he understood now that perhaps Rose was right in wanting not to bother, however he had now caused both, Thalayli and Rose, unnecessary suffering. Now due to his wishes, both rider and dragon were injured and if he did not bring about some heroic rescue then death would soon take them. Laylan ground is teeth together causing his jaw physical pain. He despised himself now for what he had done; he had pushed Rose in to trusting him, even though he knew how hard she found being around another elf. But he had let her down and betrayed her trust; again. It was as though history was repeating itself. Laylan had to thing of some terrific plan to save Rose and Thalayli; but what? Then, as though God himself had laid the thought right before the elf, Laylan knew exactly what he must do.

"May I remain here for a while; I must gather strength for I intend to seek out the dwarves."

"You may stay here Laylan, however you are forbidden to see the girl and the dragon, is that understood?"

"Yes Carman." Laylan nodded and traipsed off in to the forest leaving a paralyzed Rose and Thalayli to the mercy of the elves.

. . . .

Rose awoke to find herself high up in a tree surrounded by birch branches that formed a sort of prison cell around her. She felt weak and limp; she had no memory of what had happened, except for a blood curdling scream that still echoed in her ears.

It was dark outside and the wind whistled through the trees. She sat herself up and gazed around at the cell. She grabbed the branches and shook them hard; the tree shook but did not give way. She tried to use magic to break the branches, however the rays of light just passed straight through, not affecting the branches at all. She growled in frustration and continued to sit against a branch, gazing, out above the canopy, at the stars.

Rose stayed in the cell for three days, she grew weaker and weaker as she ate and drank nothing. She worried for Thalayli; what had become of him? She reached out with her conscience to find him but found that she could reach no further than the walls of the cage. She sat for hours just trying to find a way to penetrate the branches and find help.

It was unlike Rose to ask for help; however she knew that there was no way for her to escape the cage with out knowing the form of magic in which they had used. Had she known then she could have reversed it and gone to the aid of Thalayli. She pined for him; she cried as she missed his company, his knowledge. She pictured herself looking in to his wise, old eyes and seeing his soul behind them.

Rose could see much from just looking in to a persons eyes; she could see the truth, the lies, their fears and their joys. She valued this little and barely used her gift. She shut herself off from the world and was self focused. She worried little of others or their feelings. To Rose the only one that truly mattered was herself, after all it was her life and her world, and she was the most important person in it. In fact when she really thought about it, she didn't even care that much for Thalayli; she used to, but now her life was different, different from what it used to be. Something had changed her and she could no longer feel. She felt for no one, she did not care for anything. She felt no fear, pain, love or joy. However to say she was completely emotionless would be a lie. She still felt certain emotions; deep down; all that was needed was for them to come to the surface, though for ill or good was not knowable.

On the third day Rose heard someone approaching; as they came closer she noted that there were three people. Into view came Carman and two other elven guards that Rose recognized from her last visit to Elvendin. The guards were dressed in a dark leaf green so as to allow them to hide amongst the forest canopy with ease. They wore hats that greatly resembled large socks, which had the situation been different; Rose would have found them highly amusing. Instead however she turned her gaze to what they were holding. In their grasp were a series of ropes and a small knife. Rose eyed these objects warily, aware of what their intentions were. Carman levitated the rope from the guards hold, and directed it through the cage bars; it then wound itself rapidly around Rose's neck, wrists and ankles, proceeding to then draw her against the side of her small prison and tie her to the bars.

For a moment Rose struggled, but the rope was only drawn tighter. It was not long before the rough rope was digging in to her flesh, drawing blood and slowly cutting through the muscles of her arms and legs. The rope around her neck dug into her wind pipe causing her to gasp for breath. The pain was excruciating and as adrenaline pumped through her veins Rose's body began to shake.

"The more you struggle, the tighter the ropes will become." Carman entered the cage, flanked by the two guards. She glared in to Rose's dark eyes, and Rose glared back, her teeth grinding so as to help her bare the pain. She had stopped struggling the instant that Carman had spoke, however the ropes did not slacken, and the blood did not fail to continue flowing on to the leaven floor.

With a flick of her wrist Carman slackened the rope around Rose's neck, once again allowing her to breath. Rose hung her head slightly as the life slowly drained out of her.

"We have come to ask you a few questions Rose?"

"I know why you are here, and what you intend to ask! Though you shall never get any answers from me!" Rose's voice was coarse and the sound failed to travel very far. It appeared that the rope around her neck had caused damage to her vocal cords.

"Very well, we shall just have to do things the hard way!" Carman growled right in Rose's face; however Rose only continued to glare at the elf, and chose not to retaliate.

Carman nodded to the guard closest to her; a short middle-aged man. He appeared rather placid in nature, though there was a glint in his eye that suggested that there was a part of him that perhaps was going to enjoy what he was about to do to Rose. In his hand was a small silver knife, the blade no longer than three or four inches, the hilt was inlaid with small white, glistening diamonds. The guards approached Rose and she raised her head slightly attempting to keep the knife in sight.

"Nothing to fear of a silver knife I hope, have you?" Carman whispered in Rose's ear. "I have had my suspicions about you; ever since you returned. Now we shall see." Carman now stepped back and allowed the guards to stand before Rose.

Rose was now shaking more than ever, not through fear, but from complete and utter outrage. Her anger was welling up inside her. Once again she fought against the rope, roaring in her almighty attempt at getting free. Yet once again the ropes contracted; her head was pulled back against the cage bars as the rope around her neck tightened. The ropes bound around her wrists and ankles tightened even more; it could have appeared to an onlooker that perhaps the ropes could go no tighter. It was now hard to see where the rope ended and the flesh began. Rose screamed in anger, she felt weak from blood loss *and she failed to have any sensation or movement in her hands and feet. Tears of hate streamed down her face as she ground her teeth even harder in an attempt to stem her violent screams.*

Rose then remained still; for the second time the rope around her neck slackened, yet the other four ropes remained contracted. Carman shook her head and smirked.

"I have waited a long time for this." She nodded to the guard with the silver knife and he stepped forward so that he was now only a few inches away from Rose. She eyed the knife cautiously yet knew that should she move the ropes would tighten even more, and it felt now that the only thing left to cut through was bone. Her breathing was sharp and uneven, and still her body trembled.

The guard placed the sharp edge of the blade upon Rose's forearm, and then with one quick sweep sliced the length of her arm. Rose tried to remain still as her flesh burned; blood ran fluently across her skin and trickled on to the floor. Around the wound the skin was burnt, it smoked slightly and the smell of burning flesh emitted from her skin. She dared to turn her head to look at the wound; the skin had begun to ulcerate and was oozing a silver substance that was burning through her skin like acid.

"All these years Rose and I was right all along. Now, will you tell us how you cheated death; one part of your story has already become apparent to me; but what I wish to know is how did you escape the void? And what is your business upon the earth now? Who are you working for?" Carman was now stood right before Rose, a mere inch from her face. Rose did not answer; she just simply glared at the elf before her.

"Very well." Carman stepped aside and allowed the guard to approach Rose. The guard placed the blade upon Rose's chest, just above her bodice. As the blade touched her skin, it began to burn, smoke slowly rising from her skin. Very slowly the guard sliced in to her flesh, savoring the pain as it crossed Rose's face. Upon her skin he carved, *Hae sareth*, meaning Black Soul.

Tears streamed down Rose's face, but her body remained completely still. She relaxed and turned her head to face Carman.

Her voice barely audible she whispered hoarsely, "He'll come you know, and when he does all of hell shall rise. The world no longer belongs to you Carman. He's coming and whether you're ready or not, there's nothing you can do to stop him." Carman's face suddenly lost all color as Rose passed out. "Get her down from there; there is no point in continuing today." And with that Carman left the cage and disappeared out of sight. The two guards remained to remove the ropes that had now buried themselves deep within the flesh of Rose. As the ropes were removed her body fell limply to the ground; and there it was that she remained, the only sound that could be heard was her sharp, shallow breathing.

The short guard turned to the other as the left the tree and said, "What do you think that was about then?"

"Don't have a bloody clue I'm afraid Paul; seemed pretty important though."

"Ye, it did didn't it." And with that the two guards shrugged at each other, then disappeared out of sight.

That night Rose heard a stirring outside, the branches surrounding the cell were quivering as it appeared that someone was making their way up the tree. Shortly after the branches began moving, Rose painfully tilted her head enabling her to see a brown haired head appear from within the leaves. "Shh, let's get out of here quick before we are found." Laylan pointed his right palm at the cell and whispered, "Nofath, kerbaan herwith." The branches constructing the cell lowered and Laylan was able to clamber in to the cage. It was then that he saw Rose; a crumpled weakened body upon the ground. He slowly approached her and looked in to her face. Her eyes were barely open and her fighting spark seemed to have faded.

Laylan attempted to pick her up, but as he went to grab for her wrists he saw the scabbed wounds in her flesh. The elf tried his upmost not to be sick, as he saw the shredded ligaments and mangled flesh. He could also smell the burns from the gashes upon her arms from where the silver knife had sliced her. It was now that he saw the carving upon her chest. *Hae Sareth.* Laylan closed his eyes briefly and turned his head away; the elf then took a deep breath and hoisted Rose over his shoulder.

"Rose, we must get out of here, It won't be long before the guards come to check you."

"Where is Thalayli?" Rose's voice was barely audible, and she struggled for breath.

"He is safe but wounded. We must hurry, he has lost a lot of blood; we need to heal him as soon as possible; and we must try to heal you as well, you have lost too much blood. It's a miracle that you're still alive." Rose glared at Laylan, then gritted her teeth and rose. For a moment it was questionable as to whether her mangled ankles were going to hold her weight; however they did, and Rose took a step towards the entrance of the cage. Laylan frowned at her in total, utter disbelief.

"Are you still able to turn?" Asked Rose in a throaty whisper.

"Yes, it would save me from carrying you; but Rose, are you sure that you are strong enough"

"I'm not even going to answer that; after you" and with that Laylan frowned then leapt of the branch out of sight. Rose looked down to see a large golden eagle soaring in and out of the trees in to the distance. Rose stood twenty feet off the ground; she leapt into the air, racing towards the forest floor. In mid-flight her body changed. Fur sprouted from her skin, her hands and feet turned to paws, her arms and legs thinned and altered into small black, well-refined legs. She felt her neck tilt back and shrink into her back, her coccyx sprouted a long, fluffy tail, and her face became elongated and whiskers developed.

She landed gracefully upon the leaf covered ground. The powerful black wolf stood proud in the heart of the forest. She sniffed the air, her senses heightened, and she followed Laylan out of Elvendin.

Rose ran, dodging the ancient trees that appeared from nowhere, seemingly attempting to stop her leaving the forest. They called to her but she ignored them, their cries echoing in her mind. Her wounds throbbed and still blood oozed from the torn flesh; to an onlooker it would have seemed completely impossible for her even to be standing. As Is said many times in the world, 'if it were an animal, we'd put it down.' It was apparent that something was keeping Rose alive; something otherworldly, supernatural.

Rose had been running for several, agonizing minutes passed before she was relieved to find that the trees were beginning to thin, and she saw Laylan hovering up ahead. He had stopped over a large mound silhouetted in the blackness of the night. As Rose drew nearer she recognized the mound to be Thalayli. His left wing was crumpled beneath him and blood gushed from wounds that covered his body, arrows still protruding from his flesh. She turned back into her human form and sprinted towards the dragon, however her legs gave way and Rose crumpled in a heap beside him. She scrambled her way back up again and took in the sight before her. The moon shone down on them providing enough light for Rose to work. She began at the worst wounds; she slowly prized the arrows from the dragon's body and placed her palm over the damaged flesh, "Alhall, Keribath." The wounds slowly began to nit back together, the ligaments and tendons that were damaged could be seen mending in those wounds that were deeper.

Rose made her way up to his fine, handsome head. However it now appeared scarred and broken. The arrow still sat wedged in his left eye. Rose looked at it, a tear running down her face.

"I have let you down my friend." Rose whispered as she ran her fingers down the line of the dragon's fantastic jaw. Thalayli rumbled an answer but had no strength left to offer her a full response. Rose placed her had on the shaft of the arrow, she prepared to pull it out but found that she could not. "He is going to lose his eye, Laylan. I cannot heal this wound." Rose could see the reflection of truth within Laylan's eyes; he nodded and smiled weakly trying to encourage her.

Rose grabbed the arrow firmly, blood still gushing from her own wounds, and pulled. The arrow came easily away, however with the arrow came a dark black eye. Blood poured from Thalayli's eye socket, the nerves and blood vessels a mangled mess. Rose threw the arrow aside and began to heal the now empty black socket upon his face. After an hour of incantations and swift hand movements, the socket was clean and appeared as just a hole in Thalayli's face. His once grand, handsome face was now no more than a scarred, mutilated shadow of what it used to be. There was no spark, no glint of hope that things would get better. It now occurred to Rose that to herself, and many others, Thalayli's majestic and mysterious eyes held more than just beauty. They held a ray of hope that even when times are dark, there is always a star to guide us, no matter where we are. Now there was nothing, no way forward. The darkened dragon gazed with one eye into Rose's face.

Thank you, it is for the best.

Rose did not answer, but poured her whole heart and soul in to Thalayli. He felt her love for him, and her gratitude that he had not blamed her for the loss of his eye.

Slowly Thalayli rose to his feet, his wounds now fully healed; he was still weak and wobbled slightly as he regained his balance. He twisted his neck to look at Rose and Laylan, *Laylan are you able to heal Rose's wounds?*

"I am sorry Rose, Thalayli; I am not as powerful as you. I do not have the strength to heal you."

Laylan hung his head as though suffering from a great shame.

"It is no matter Laylan, I shall heal myself as we travel; for I fear if we linger here much longer then we are sure to be found." Rose clambered clumsily up Thalayli's shoulder, and sat in her usual place just behind his wither, leaning against one of the many tines upon his back. Laylan sat between the two tines behind her.

Shall we go then? Thalayli turned his snake like neck so as to look at the two beings sat upon his back.

"Are you strong enough Thalayli?" asked Laylan.

"He will not use his strength, he shall use mine." Rose gazed up in to the hollow socket that used to hold a proud, wise eye. Thalayli appeared lost, weak; it seemed he had lost more than just his eye; it seemed as if his soul was now enveloped by darkness. Rose closed her eyes and reached out with her conscience in an attempt to find it, however all she found was darkness.

And so it was that the girl and the elf sat astride the dragons back, and with one swift movement Thalayli leapt in to the sky.

Chapter 10

A Power Lies Within

"There is a hero in all of us; we can all reach out and help a soul in need. But in some the hero lies deep, and it can be questioned as to whether or not a hero lies within them at all. However they need to embrace the chances in which they are given to do the right thing; and draw the hero from its slumber."

Sarabie awoke the following morning after being fully revived from her tiresome journey. She was totally, emotionally exhausted. Her emotions seemed to have overpowered her physical exhaustion as all that was apparent to her conscience were her emotions. It was clear that Sarabie's feelings had taken over her being; however was it possible for her to gain control of these emotions. It was known to her that she had distinct feelings for Laylan. She hadn't known it until now. That night she had dreamt of the handsome young elf, and this had therefore been playing on her mind all morning. His face, his muscular yet slender body seemed to be constantly reflected upon everywhere in which she gazed.

Sarabie tried to blank these feelings; she rose from her leaven bed and walked over to Nenamis and sat beside him waiting for him to wake. She was only sat there momentarily as he had sensed her approaching, though thought that perhaps Sarabie would find it comforting to lay by his side for a while. Of course he was right; in all his wisdom, Nenamis knew the psychology behind a human's action's; therefore he knew that when it came to Sarabie he must tread very carefully, as after all he knew that she was the kingdoms only hope.

So after a few minutes of silence between the girl and the dragon, Nenamis raised his huge head and slowly turned it to look at Sarabie.

Good morning, he said slowly, slightly inclining his head towards her as he did so.

Ye, it is. Everything is going to be so different. Sarabie leant on Nenamis's overly large flank; he seemed to hum in response to her elevated feeling of joy at her new improved circumstances.

Even when Nenamis was tucked away in his egg, deep in the heart of the castle, he could still sense Sarabie's emotions. He had noticed the dramatic change in her, now she could finally come out of this shell in which she had created and now at last enjoy her life. However there were a couple of things about Sarabie that caused Nenamis to have doubts in his mind as to whether or not the prophecy regarded her. The dragon sensed a darkness within her which he felt himself unable to trust. He chose to ignore this, and wait to see what the elves would have to say about Sarabie's future.

It was a short while later when an elf clambered up to Sarabie's tree house. She heard a rap at the door and rose from her snoozing position beside Nenamis. She waddled over to the hung branches that blocked off the entrance to her tree house. Sarabie lazily pushed aside the leaves and saw before her a young elf no older than herself.

"Hi." Sarabie said, nervously. She looked the elf up and down subconsciously taking in his scruffy black hair, pale nervous face and dark blue eyes.

The elf bowed low and greeted Sarabie, "Good morning Miss; your tutor awaits you in the quiet glen. I am here to guide you to him." The elf bowed again. Sarabie unaware of how to respond to the elf bowed back and replied, "Thank you."

Nenamis turned his head lethargically to gaze at the elf. The young boy noticed the dragon gazing at him and averted his gaze instantly. Looking at his shoes the elf bowed even lower than he had previously. "It is a great honor to finally meet you, Niver Nenamis." The grand dragon simply inclined his head in response, and then continued to doze.

"I will give you a few minutes to prepare yourself Miss."

"Thank you," answered Sarabie. The elf turned and retreated back down the tree steps and waited at the base of the tree. Sarabie walked back in to the tree house and sat beside Nenamis.

What do you think we will be doing today?

I don't know, answered the dragon. *The sooner you dress, the sooner we will find out.*

Sarabie was currently dressed in just a tunic which stopped several inches above the knee; it was green in color and had been tied at the waist by a piece of brown cord. It was now that it occurred to Sarabie why the young male elf had been so nervous. Sarabie had removed the rest of her garments as she felt that sleeping in them would be rather uncomfortable, and the elves were yet to provide her with any other form of garments fit for sleeping in.

So Sarabie quickly dressed and clambered out of the tree house. Nenamis landed by her side as he flew down from the tree tops. The young elf bowed again and said "Please follow me."

Sarabie and Nenamis followed the elf; it now occurred to Sarabie that she did not know the elf's name, however just as she went to ask him he seemed to read her mind and turned to her and said, "My name is Raphael; it is now my job to serve you and make sure that you and Niver Nenamis are comfortable."

"That is very kind of you, thank you." Sarabie was finding it hard to converse with Raphael; she seemed unable to think of anything to say to him. It felt to her as though she was beneath him and that she should not be talking to him at all. Nenamis picked up on this instantly. He became aware now of how being shut away all her life had affected Sarabie. All her life she had had no human interaction, in fact she had no interaction with another living being at all. The dragon sensed her lack in self confidence, sensed her fear and felt her urge to simply turn around, walk back to the tree house and remain there, alone, for the rest of her life. This made Nenamis feel sympathy towards Sarabie, however he made sure to bury this emotion, along with his knowledge of Sarabie's darker side; Nenamis knew that this sort of knowledge would crush Sarabie even more and destroy the last ray of self confidence she had left.

After only a few minutes the trio reached a large open glen. The sky was a bright blue with out a single cloud visible. The trees around the glen consisted of pine and fir, and the only flower visible was a lone silver snowdrop. Beside the single flower sat Laylan, he was cross legged, his hands resting on his knees and his eyes were lightly closed. As the threesome entered the glen Laylan opened his eyes and gestured for Sarabie to sit beside him. She did as she was told and Nenamis sat himself by her side, taking up a considerable amount of the glen.

Laylan nodded to Raphael, who then made a swift exit.

Sarabie felt out of place sat beside the elf; she could sense Laylan's magical energy and the strength that resided within him. This made her feel small, and insignificant.

"We will start by building your self-confidence. Most things in life come from believing you can achieve it rather than just trying to achieve it." Laylan spoke in a calm and relaxed voice. He closed his eyes again then continued to speak.

"Close your eyes. Imagine the earth with out any life upon it. There is no existence, just the world; untouched by man, it is just as the lord created it. There are vast open valleys, broad unpolluted rivers, and forests that seem unending.

'Then upon the Earth, the lord places a group of souls. He gives them nothing except the world around them. With the world they may do as they wish, however each persons wish is different. Now, instead of sorting out their issues in a civilized manner, they argue and fights begin, leading to wars. Then before you, you witness the souls upon the Earth going their separate ways and the three races are created; the elves, the dwarves and the humans."

"Why did they argue?" Sarabie asked as she listened intently to Laylan's every word.

"The Lord gave us all lessons to learn. You see, when he created Earth, he also created heaven; heaven is a place of peace and ecstasy. However to keep heaven pure the Lord created lessons in which we had to learn whilst we were here on Earth. He did not tell us what these lessons were, but when a lesson was learnt you would have a feeling of enlightenment. So when you died, and all the lessons had been learnt you proceeded to heaven"

"What happened if you died and had failed to learn all of the lessons?"

"Then it was, that you were reborn again upon the Earth. This cycle would continue until all the lessons were learnt. This is one of the reasons why the races split, some became frustrated that they could not learn the lessons laid down, and eventually completely forgot about the lessons and so became stuck in a never ending loop of life and death. This race is called the Dwarves.

'The humans sought dominance; this is why they are stuck in the life and death loop. They turned against the Lord and what he had given them."

"What had he given them?"

"For one he had given them life. But when the humans stayed true to the Lord, yet still failed to learn all off the lessons, the Lord placed some of their souls in the bodies of animals. The idea of this was to help them learn the lessons of life from a different perspective; the Lord thought perhaps that this would work. Now those humans who had been reborn with the body of an animal quickly learnt all of the lessons and when they died went to heaven. However the humans who remained in their human bodies tried to dominate the animals and so they turned away from the Lord. They even began to find other reasons as to why they were here; reasons that did not include the Creator at all."

"What about the elves?"

"The elves made many mistakes. We, I fear, are perhaps the worst race. There are a few elves, about a thousand, who have been on the Earth since the beginning of time, everyone else has been reborn. The elves had learnt all of the lessons laid down by the Lord, but instead of passing on to heaven they chose to come back to the Earth and help guide those who were still yet to learn the lessons of life. The Lord decided to aid the elves by granting them the secret of magic. However people refused the help of the elves believing them to have been sent by an evil power. The elves asked for the help of the Lord, however he refused saying that he had already helped them enough; this of course angered the elves, and together they chose to turn their backs on the Lord. By making this decision they chose to remain upon the Earth for an eternity. Of course elves are immortal, but should they circum to an injury then death can not be helped. This is when elves are born. I was reborn only sixteen years ago, however in my life before I was stabbed in the back by my best friend whilst on the battle field. I remember everything, right back to the beginning."

"So you can't ever die?"

"Yes and no, the Lord is the only one who can chose whether we are accepted in to heaven."

"What made the humans and the dwarves think that there was an evil power?"

"Well we do not know where the evil power came from but we do know that it does exist. The evil power used to speak to those people who were struggling to learn life's lessons. He would offer them a way out, trick those in to thinking that he could be trusted and that his way was right and everyone else's way was wrong. We have a theory that he may be an elf that went to far in the mission to forget The Lord; however we do not know how he is able to manipulate people in such a way. Whatever he is, one day he will be stopped; but whoever is destined to stop him will have to be incredibly powerful. Luckily the one to defeat him will not be you as it has yet to be prophesized. So we can be grateful to the lord for that.

'Now do you have any more questions?"

Sarabie shook her head vigorously. However Nenamis lifted his head from the grass and said,

Where did the dragons come from?

The dragons come from different worlds, they do not remember anything from their previous world but they understand that it is their job to protect the world in which they are in.

What do you mean by different worlds? And how do you know all of this?

I know because I saw the coming of the dragons. They came when the elves first turned their backs on the Lord. God hoped that the dragons would be powerful enough to over turn the elves decision and show the dwarves and the humans the way. However this only made the races argue more, and more wars broke out. The dragons went in to hiding. I remember speaking to the Lord of the dragons, and he said to me once, 'We respect every living creature's choices and opinions; however there are better places than here and there are better times than now. This is why the Lord created us. It is our job to help put things right, no matter what world, no matter what species; because there are better places than here, and better times than now.'"

Nenamis hummed in gratitude in having his question answered so adequately.

"If the elves are that old how do they remember everything?" Sarabie asked as she stroked the flower in front of her.

"That is a wise question. There is a book; it is called Ce Libera et Viscis. This is elvish for the book of time. The book is ancient; it has been in our possession since the world began. However its pages are complete and it is apparent to us that this book is a foretelling of all that is to be in this world, right up until the end of time. There are many secrets of the book that I believe we have not mastered, you see, the book changes. It is not known to us yet how or why it changes, but it does. The book is kept safe by the Custolis el Posteres, the keeper of the future. He is the only one trusted with the book; the majority of the elven race do not even know who the Custolis el Posteres is; which is the best way. You see, the book holds all, and in the wrong hands the entire future of the Earth could be in jeopardy." Laylan now noticed how Sarabie was playing with the snowdrop. He placed his hand upon hers and slowly moved her hand aside. He then gently removed the flower from its stalk. The elf closed his eyes and drew his hand over the flower. A faint glow seemed to emit from the palm of his right hand and was absorbed by the flowers petals. Laylan gently placed the snowdrop back on its stalk and it seemed to merge together, fixing itself so that the flower and stalk were once again whole. Laylan withdrew his hands and Sarabie noticed the change in the snowdrop. It was no longer white. The petals were now bright silver and the flower itself seemed to radiate an energy of its own.

"That's amazing; how did you do that?" Sarabie gasped, gawping at the now glowing flower.

"Magic and a lot of love and respect for the Earth. It's all about the manipulation of energies. You will learn, for I will teach you. It is all part of you training. Now you may go and explore Elvendin, do you wish for Raphael to guide you?"

"No I think I shall be ok. I have Nenamis for company."

"Very well; however I will have him come find you at dinner. There is to be a feast in your honor."

Laylan rose and bowed low to Nenamis. "I shall see you at the feast." And with that the young, handsome elf turned and strode out of the glen.

CHAPTER 11

The Wonders Of The World

'The future can be just as haunting as the past. Live your life a quarter of a mile at a time, tomorrow might never come.'

S ARABIE AND NENAMIS walked through Elvendin happily chatting to each other about their surroundings. All around them were silver birch trees, fir and pine trees and some various other trees that Sarabie did not know the names of. Each living thing, whether plant, or animal, all seemed to radiate joy and contemptment. Sarabie had never seen anything like it. Everyone and everything seemed to thoroughly enjoy being on the Earth. This in a way made Sarabie sad. She had never known joy before; and in a way she resented all of the beings around her. She did not understand why she had been denied the simple pleasures of freedom when all of the creatures around her had lived a life of luxury, being able to do as they pleased. Nenamis sensed this and chose to confront her and see if he could alter her way of seeing things.

Sarabie, everything you have seen and everything that has been done to you has only made you stronger. You feel that no one out there was as hard done by as you were however, there are those out there that are being tortured and abused, starved and deprived of everything. You were, but then you were saved. What about those people that have not been saved, those who will die not knowing anything different than the four walls that have imprisoned them for their entire life. The troubles in which you have seen in your life make you able to help those who are going through similar troubles. You are able to understand how they feel, you can sympathies. This is your gift and with it you will be able to help others through their troubles. You must lend them your strength, by doing this you are providing them with a ray of hope that will help to keep them fighting.

Nenamis lowered his head and turned to look in to Sarabie's eyes. *I believe Sarabie, that you could save the world.*

Sarabie hung her head now feeling guilty about her previous emotions. She looked about her and began to appreciate her surroundings. If it were not for Nenamis, Sky and Laylan she would not be here, and for that she was truly grateful.

Dusk was now falling and it was not long before she was approached by Raphael. Now he was garbed in a rich magenta robe that was fastened by a golden broach in the shape of a star. His tunic and breeches were also of a matching color and were made of soft velvet. He bowed low when he reached them; he then proceeded to greet them.

"Sarabie, Niver Nenamis. I hope your day has been most plesentful, and that you have learnt a great amount from Master Laylan. I appreciate that you are having a good time exploring the forest, however you are requested to change your clothing and attend a grand feast which we have prepared especially for you and Niver Nenamis. Would you please care to attend?"

Sarabie smiled then replied, "I would be honored."

Raphael bowed low then said, "I shall meet you at the trunk of your tree in an hour." He inclined his head then strode away purposefully.

Nenamis turned to look at Sarabie, *I guess we had better fly to the tree; we want as much time as possible for you to get ready.* The great dragon smiled down at the girl. Sarabie clambered clumsily on to his back which now stood a good ten feet of the ground. The only way in which she could climb upon him was to use his elbow as a step. This apparently was not contested by Nenamis as instead he hummed quietly.

The red dragon took off and soared over the forest canopy. They were flying for only a matter of seconds before he dived back in to the forest and landed neatly on the over hang of the tree house. Sarabie jumped off awkwardly and landed heavily upon the branch. Nenamis seemed to smile at her and said, *it will get easier I think. I feel we both still have a lot to learn.*

Nenamis? How is it that you knew exactly where to land, and how far to fly?

It is one of the many gifts of the dragons, photographic memory. I can picture anything in which I have seen before in my minds eye. It is a marvelous gift. Of course, you are also blessed with this gift due to the linking of our minds. Anything you wish to see, you may see through my mind. I will show you.

Sarabie felt Nenamis reaching out towards her with his conscience. It felt like something pushing softly at the inside of her head. *Open your mind* said the wizened dragon.

Sarabie seemed to understand and dropped all of the other thoughts that had been loitering within her mind. She allowed his mind to fully merge with hers.

At once Sarabie became fully aware of everything around her; it was as though all of her senses had been heightened. The bird song, the rustle of the trees, the scent of the underground, and even the taste of the air upon her lips; it all seemed so clear to her now.

Then Nenamis created an image. Sarabie could feel him developing the picture with in his conscience. She closed her eyes and watched as an image appeared right before her; it appeared so real that it was as though she were really there. She saw before her the glen in which she had sat with Laylan earlier on that day. The scene was so real in fact, that Sarabie could feel the wind tickling every pore upon her face, and each hair upon her head. She could scent the lone snowdrop within the glen; even sense its energy as she stood many yards away from it. Everything felt to her now so alive. So much information flooded Sarabie's mind, yet it did not seem to overwhelm her; it felt to her as though this was how life should be.

Slowly the image began to fade. The scents, sounds and sight ebbing away. Sarabie opened her eyes and gazed at the dragon. It then became clear to her that she could still sense every minuet feeling about her. It was as though her senses had been heightened, even with out Nenamis's input. The dragon looked down at the girl and said softly, *We are becoming closer, we are part of each other.* Nenamis lowered his great nose towards Sarabie's face and blew softly on her skin.

We will never be parted Nenamis, never. I will guard you with my life and make sure that no harm ever comes to you.

As I will also guard you Sarabie.

Sarabie and Nenamis walked into the tree house to find a beautiful satin dress laid upon the bed. It was a rich burgundy in color and appeared to be long in length. Sarabie quickly washed using a bowl of warm water that had been set aside for her and slipped in to the dress. It was fairly low cut and was of a halter neck design. Also laid upon the bed was a fur shawl. It was soft to the touch but it was apparent that it was not the coat of an animal. Lastly, Sarabie placed her dainty feet in to a pair of black leather sandals that were then covered by the length of the dress.

After a few minutes of making sure that she looked ok, Sarabie clambered on to Nenamis's back and together they flew down to the base of the tree.

Raphael stood quietly there waiting for them in no apparent hurry. He ambled up to them and said, "Would you mind me following?" he staggered slightly. "I'm 'erribly 'orry. Would you mind following me?"

Sarabie dismounted Nenamis and turned to smile at the dragon. He hummed in response then continued to follow the tottery elf.

"I must apologies, for you see this is a day of celebration. Therefore, of course completely 'ceptable, I have hit the early a little mead."

Sarabie grinned and answered, "That is quite alright Mr Raphael, sir."

Raphael stopped and turned to face the girl and the dragon.

"You are kind too far. You do not deserve the fate that awaits you. Definitely not."

"What, what do you mean, I don't deserve the fate that awaits me?" Sarabie took a step forwards as she felt Nenamis's questioning thoughts merging with hers.

"Oh no, I have said far too much. My place it is not." The elf went to bow low however only found himself hitting the ground with a dull thud. He did not make any attempt to get up, in fact he did not move at all. The only way in which it could be told that the fellow was still alive was by the loud snores that were now erupting from his crow shaped nose.

Well it's now apparent that our guide is unconscious. Nenamis's comment made Sarabie's heart lighten slightly, and both herself and the dragon had chosen to ignore all comments said by the elf adhering to the fact that he was clearly drunk.

Well how are we going to find our way to the feast now? Actually no matter.
Just as Sarabie had began her statement she had heard a commotion
slightly further down the path. The pair abandoned the elf and followed
the path forward. They had silently agreed that Raphael would be fine
except for a headache in the morning.

It was not long before Sarabie and Nenamis had entered a large
clearing filled with elves. Some were sat upon large mushrooms, or
boulders eating overly large plates of every type of food you could
possibly imagine, other elves were dancing to a haunting tune played by
an orchestra of elves at the far side of the clearing, and the remainder
of the elves were stood to the clearings edges looking nervous and
apprehensive.

However the girl and the dragon were not given long to take in
their surroundings for they had quite suddenly been swarmed with;
pats on the back, hand shakes and many cheers of delight at their
presence. After what seemed like an age of not quite knowing how
to react, Sarabie saw Carman manage to fight her way through the
crowd.

"I am terribly sorry if you felt pressured Sarabie, they are just
glad that at last the world may now stand a chance at peace; and, of
course, it is all down to you. Now I do hope that hasn't pressurized
you too much. Please sit with us in the glen where we may toast to
your coming." It was at this point that the elven leader turned to face
Nenamis. "And you to of course Niver Nenamis."

The crowd of elves parted slowly and begrudgingly, all of them
still trying to touch Sarabie and Nenamis. At the far side of the glen
Carman sat herself crossed legged upon the mossy earth. She then
gestured for Sarabie and Nenamis to do the same. Then in unison the
other elves copied so that there was one huge circle around the glen.

Once everyone was seated Carman began to speak, however
Sarabie noted not what she was saying, as it had now come to her
attention that Laylan was not present. She scouted the circle in search
of his sharp, fine face; however it was no where to be seen.

It must then have been that Carman noticed Sarabie's lack of
attention for she now chose to direct her speech at her.

"We must thank you Sarabie. It is told that your life is dedicated to
that of peace, and for that we are truly grateful. And for all of those
barriers in which you must cross to achieve your goal we will be right

there beside you; any sacrifice that you may have to make will also be our own. I want you to always remember that. We will always, no matter what hard times come to pass we will always be beside you."

Now Nenamis, being of higher intelligence than the majority of the folk in the glen, if not all of them, noted that perhaps Carman was trying to make a hidden remark.

Sarabie, there is something I do not trust about Carman, and where is Laylan?

You noticed that too huh? I do not know but I really don't wish to be at this feast thing for too long. Carman scares me, I just don't like her. It is as though she expects me to do something that perhaps is not for the sole purpose of peace. I don't know what it is but I don't feel safe around her.

Nenamis chose not to answer fully, he was now far to engrossed in the food that was now being brought in to the centre of the glen. Laid before the dragon now was an entire deer, its brown coat rippling in the twilight. Nenamis cracked his neck left and right, then did not hesitate to rip the carcass open and chomp upon the deer's raw flesh.

Now this in any normal circumstance would probably have turned one's stomach inside out. However laid before Sarabie and the rest of the elves was the most fantastic feast that Sarabie had ever laid eyes upon. There were a huge variety of fruits and vegetables that she was sure could not possibly exist due to their bight coloring and peculiar shapes.

"Carman, what is this called?" Sarabie now pointed at a fluorescent pink ball with rubber like spikes upon its surface.

"We call it a fluerec fruit. It is from the far mountains up north where the dwarves live. But Sarabie do not eat the skin, you must remove it before eating."

Sarabie paused just before the fruit was about to enter her mouth. She looked at it now incredibly confused as to how she was supposed to remove the skin without using her teeth. Carman took the fruit from Sarabie's hand and began to pull at one of the many spikes situated at what appeared to be the top of the fruit. As she pulled the entire skin of the fruit seemed to fall away leaving a soft fleshy centre.

Carman smiled and handed the fluerec back to Sarabie. As Sarabie bit in to the fruit her mouth seemed to erupt with a huge variety of flavors and sensations. Her tongue seemed to be fizzing and she could taste fresh ripe cherries and strawberries, though there was a sweet taste there that she failed to compare to anything she had ever eaten.

After a good hour or so of face stuffing, the glen rapidly began to fill with excited chatter. Sarabie looked about her to see if there was anything worth getting excited about, then she noticed where all of the other elves were looking. Stood deep in the shadows to one side of the glen stood Laylan. He did not move forward or make any acknowledgement that he was being pointed at and talked about. He caught Sarabie's eye, then turned and strode of into the darkness.

Sarabie was just about to question Nenamis when, *I saw him as well, perhaps we can ask him tomorrow what is going on. It seems of yet that he does not like to be with other elves.*

Hmmm . . .

Carman now stood up and walked to the centre of the glen. She raised both arms up in to the air, her palms facing skyward. The sun was now low in the sky and its color was no longer its normal dull blue, it was now a livid purple with streaks of pink and orange. As Carman stood there in the heart of the circle she seemed to begin to glow. The entire glen seemed to be holding its breath, even the birds and the trees. Then, from now where, a bright, glowing orb of yellow light erupted in the palms of Carman's hands. It rose in to the air and hung about two feet above her head. There it grew in diameter until it appeared like a small sun lighting the clearing.

Carman stepped away from the energy ball and nodded to the orchestra. The elves rose and one by one they began to dance. They danced as though they were part of the music. They danced in time with one another, and they danced as if there was no need ever to stop.

I do not feel comfortable here, Sarabie told Nenamis. But before he had chance to answer Raphael had appeared out of nowhere, apparently now wide awake and full of energy.

"Come with me, you must try some mead." The elf dragged her to a corner and forced a wooden cup in to her hand. A stout little elf then approached her rolling a small barrel.

"Zee, barr'el iz not for you, it iz for zee dragon." However Nenamis took one sniff of the mead and turned his nose up.

I don't know about everyone else in this glen, but I would rather still have full control of my mind and body, thank you.

However it was doubtful as to whether or not his statement was heard for Sarabie had been dragged here and there by a number of different elves, with numerous different beverages forced down her neck.

Nenamis chose now to sit at the side of the glen and oversee the goings on. As long as he was there Sarabie was safe.

And so the night went on, and the elves danced, the music played and the moon went back in to hiding. It was not until the sun began to rise again that the elves slowed the proceedings. Sarabie was now fast asleep leant against Nenamis's side, and the majority of the elves were now sprawled in a similar fashion to that of Raphael when he had come to escort Sarabie and Nenamis to the feast.

Nenamis sat beside Sarabie listening to her breathing, feeling her life force and energy beside his. He felt the stillness that now resided in the glen. Carman's energy ball had now faded and gone and he was pretty sure that all of the food and mead was now gone as well.

It must have been around midday when folk started coming around. There were many groans and stifled mutters that told Nenamis that everyone was perhaps not feeling their best. He hummed, pleased with his good judgment on not drinking.

He felt Sarabie stir beside him and he gently brushed her head with his nose.

"Urrrrrrr, meh." Sarabie turned to face Nenamis and he smiled down at her.

And how do you feel this fine day?

Like my heads being crushed and I'm being spun round at a hundred miles an hour.

Nenamis just continued to smile at her as he gently helped her on to his back. Within minutes Sarabie and Nenamis were back at the tree house where they were looking forward to snuggling up together in Nenamis's sunken bed. However it was not to be as when they entered the tree house, they were not alone.

Laylan stood at the far side of the tree house gazing in the direction of Sarabie and Nenamis.

"How was the feast?" he said blankly. Sarabie felt his lack of emotion behind this question and chose to answer cautiously.

"It was ok thank you. However I think it would have been better perhaps if you had been there."

Laylan paused briefly then replied, "I am sorry I did not attend, there were other matters in which I had to attend to."

"But, I saw you. You were stood at the edge of the glen. Why didn't you come over?"

"There are some elves that I do not fully get along with. I thought it best if problems did not arise during your feast as I did not wish to ruin the celebration of you and Nenamis. Now please do not question me any further. I as your master have my own rights to remain silent about matters in which I believe do not concern contemplation by you." Laylan seemed to have grown slightly in stature and appeared perhaps more intimidating and foreboding than normal. This then caused Sarabie to retreated and ask no further questions; her respect for the elf would not allow it.

"Now I am afraid to say that even though you are not feeling your best, you still required to join me in the glen for our usual training session." Laylan did look rather apologetic as he said this, however he continued to open the door and begin to walk out.

"I shall meet you in the glen in ten minutes." And with that he walked through the vines and disappeared out of view.

"Great," Sarabie gasped as she collapsed on her bed. "I have a stinking head ache and feel as though my stomach has been turned inside out." Nenamis knowing that this was not aimed at him just hummed and sat himself beside her.

If we are to meet Laylan in ten minutes then I suggest that you change from your attire and we make our way down to the glen.

Sarabie chose not to answer the dragon; instead she just rose and changed in to her tunic and leggings. With much difficulty she pulled on her leather boots tied her hair back and clambered upon Nenamis's back. The dragon strode over to the balcony and rapidly took flight. Within minutes they arrived at their destination.

Laylan was sat cross legged by the single snowdrop and seemed to be in a deep medative state. Sarabie silently slipped from the dragons back and approached Laylan. He did not respond to her presence just simply remained motionless. Used to Laylan's bizarre ways the girl opted to sit opposite him in a similar position. She looked upon the elf for a while, but still he did not move. It was as this point that Sarabie chose to close her eyes and fall in to herself. She felt that perhaps hiding in her conscience would allow her to escape the churning, weak feeling in her stomach. Sarabie had been sat like this for only a matter of minutes when she felt Laylan take her hands in his. Immediately she felt a warm sensation in her right hand. To her it's was as though warm water was being poured on to the palm of her hand. Her left hand however was ice cold, and felt as though the coldness was being drawn through her body and out through her palm. Soon after these sensations began Sarabie began to feel light and all pain that she had felt before had now gone; this included her headache.

The pair sat like this for several hours. Neither of them even flinching; they were now completely absorbed in what they were doing, yet they both felt entirely free. When Laylan withdrew his hands from hers, Sarabie opened her eyes to see that the elf had done the same.

"This Sarabie is what I will be teaching you today; the manipulation of energy."

Sarabie fully understood what Laylan had meant by this. He was going to teach her how to reshape and alter the energies around her; in more simple terms, magic.

"Before you is a snowdrop." Laylan inclined his head to the right where the lone snowdrop was growing. "Today I wish for you to change the snowdrop, add to its energy and make it grow." Sarabie looked from Laylan to the snowdrop and back again.

"Now Sarabie I want you to follow my instruction and listen very carefully to what I am saying. It may be that you do not achieve any change in the snowdrop today, but with practice your power will grow.'

'Now with your mind reach out to the snowdrop, feel its energy with your conscience." Laylan paused for a moment to give her chance to accomplish what he had instructed. However before he had chance to give her the next instruction the elf noticed that the small white flower was now glowing silver. It was now emitting a light of its own. It seemed to glow radiant in the sunlight and slowly it began to grow. After a short time of perhaps only half a minute the flower had reached almost ten inches in height. The stem of the snowdrop was now glittering gold and the petals where a glistening silver. The flower stopped growing and Sarabie turned her attention back to Laylan.

At first Laylan was clearly lost for words. However he then smiled and looked at Sarabie.

"You have a fantastic heart, for it takes a great amount of love for the world to create something so beautiful. Only one with a pure soul can create such beauty. You truly are blessed with a gift, and I now know that you are the one of whom is spoken of in the prophecy. The Lord has delivered you to us, and for that I truly am grateful." Laylan bowed his head as he spoke.

As this was transpiring, Nenamis sat at the edge of the glen humming. He felt Sarabie's joy at having created something so marvelous; he could feel her growing and knew that it would not be long before they were called upon to make the world a better place.

I'm going to do it Nenamis, we're going to save the world.

CHAPTER 12

Is It To Late To Repent?

"However much I strive to know everything, however hard I try, I will always know nothing."

D EAN WAS BEGINNING, at last, to feel as though perhaps what he was doing was wrong. Now it could be said that the fact that he still had to contemplate as to whether or not he was in the right or the wrong just showed how big his ego must have been and how his own ignorance clouded his judgment. To others it may seem impossible to understand the emotions being suffered by Dean at this moment in time. He was of course experiencing the rush of being the leader of a huge army that now consisted of several thousand men and a good few hundred prisoners. He felt powerful and important, every man around him feared or respected him; of course Dean believed that they obeyed him through respect when realistically they brought about his orders through fear for their families lives.

Dean also had a feeling of elation at being in his own charge and not having to look after any one else. He had no one nagging him or annoying him in any way; for all the soldiers feared making any remark or stepping out of line. Dean could do exactly as he pleased, he felt higher, mightier, and superior to all other beings.

But alongside these feelings Dean felt lonely. He had no friends amongst the soldiers, no one to talk to. Not a single person spoke to him except to relay information, and even that would be brief. This was where Jack came in. Dean thought that once he had ditched Jack, then he would be able to move on and forget about him. However this now seemed an impossible task.

It was now at this point in time that Dean contemplated looking for his brother. His plan would then be to ask his brothers forgiveness and then to carry about his duty. Now it would of course be clear to most other people with less hippo sized ego's that Jack would reject Dean's apology; especially when Jack had just received a better offer elsewhere. However Dean still believed that Jack was beneath him and that should he find his brother then Jack would surely step back in line and follow his brother's orders.

And so it was that Dean made a promise to himself that once the war was over he would find Jack and everything would carry on as it was before, except of course, Dean himself would be sitting at Karbith's right hand side. However Dean knew that he would need a servant, so who better to serve him than his own little brother.

The army had now reached a small village. It was only a matter of minutes before the village had been completely surrounded by horses and soldiers. Dean entered the congregation of cottages and sat astride his horse as he barked orders up at the people looking out of their windows with pale faces.

"I Dean, Master of the Kings army, demand that all men between the ages of sixteen and forty leave their families and join us in the fight against evil. Offer your life for our cause and you will be greatly rewarded; your families shall live."

It was not long before another thirty men had joined the army. They were now mounted on either their own horses or horses taken from the village. All of the men looked nervous and they kept looking back at the families in which they were leaving behind. From the midst of villagers appeared a small girl running towards Dean. She could have been now older than six. She grabbed at Deans horse causing it to stop, then she pulled at his leg as this was all she could reach. Her hair was blonde and curly and her eyes were of the deepest blue. Her mother was calling for her but the little girl ignored her and continued to look up in to Dean's face.

"Please don't take my Daddy and my brother. Please." She pleaded to Dean, tears streaming down her face. "Please don't take them to die?!"

Dean drew his sword and without a second thought slit her throat. The girl's body lay limp on the ground, and all that could be heard were her mother's screams.

Chapter 13

The Breaking Of A Soul

"It takes courage to change what can be changed
It takes patience when things can not be changed
But it takes knowledge to know the difference"

SARABIE SAT CROSSED legged in a quite shady glen; Laylan sat before her in the same position. Sarabie was now sixteen, her features were more predominant and with age had come elegance. She appeared wise, and at one with the world around her.

"Keep your mind open, listen to the songs around you; everything has a voice. Empty all other thoughts from your head, and be open to your surroundings." Sarabie did not respond, which Laylan deemed quite expectable, due to the fact that had she been listening to him then she would have been doing the exercise completely wrong.

Laylan rose and left Sarabie sat in the glen. She showed no signs of having noticed his absence, and she continued to sit there in silence, deep in a trance within which she had complete awareness of her surroundings.

Late in to the evening Laylan returned to the glen. Sarabie was still sat in the same position, seemingly completely unaware of the time of day.

You may rise now; I believe you have mastered the art of opening your mind.

Sarabie opened her eyes and gazed up at Laylan. "I have never heard the world so clearly before."

"It takes a lot of patience to be able to see the world for what it really is. You have come along way since you came here three years ago. Now, please, tell me what you heard."

"A war approaches, a final war that will meet a terrible end; there is evil on the air, the trees are whispering a warning; the earth it breaths, there is a fire deep within its heart, like a dragon; there is acceptance too, as though the world just floats along never straying from its path; the air around us tells us much too, it answers any question we ask; I feel that we are all here for a reason, a purpose."

"Well done, now I think we can finish for today."

"Wait! There are still some things I want to discuss."

"Ok, fire away."

"Why was the world created?"

"Have you not answered that through your meditation?"

"Well we were all created to learn things."

"Go on . . ."

"The lord, he put us here to learn lessons so that we would find peace and would therefore only bring peace to his kingdom when we are ready to move on." Laylan gazed at Sarabie lovingly.

"You have learnt more than I could have hoped for."

"But that's not what I'm here for is it?"

"What do you mean?"

"I'm here for something else; to do something. I don't think utopia is a place for me."

"My dear Sarabie; utopia is a place for all of those that find peace."

It was then that Sarabie spoke to Nenamis. *I don't feel I shall ever find peace.*

I can feel that inside of you. However no one lives here for ever, every one moves on; no one feels the same for ever.

"Anyway, with your meditation and your magic moving forward so fast, it will not be long before you over take me. Now I have just remembered what I asked you to do last night."

"I did as you said; watch." Sarabie directed the palm of her hand towards a large oak tree at the side of the glen. As she did so the tree began to glow golden. It then began to grow, taller wider; and when she stopped the tree continued to glow for a few more minutes.

"That's amazing Sarabie; growing, lifting, healing, there is little left for you to learn. You are ready for whatever is to come." Laylan bowed then said, "Now good night to you."

Sarabie bowed back then turned to Nenamis. She mounted the dragon and together they flew off in to the night.

. . . .

"Well?"

"It is worst than we thought, Carman; she is more powerful than any of us; if she chooses to disobey your orders there is nothing we can do. She is a strong person, she has been with us for three years now, and her training is almost complete." Laylan and Carman sat on the boulder bench gazing at the snowdrops as they glowed under the moonlight.

"Then it is up to you to make sure that she stays on our side."

"How?" Laylan asked this half-heartedly.

"Any way you can, I want you to poison her against the dwarves and the humans. Remind her of her past, and tell her where she came from, she must know the truth."

"Could the truth not push her in the wrong direction?"

"Only tell her what she needs to know for our cause."

"Lie to her?"

"No, tell her the truth just not all of it."

. . . .

Sarabie sat outside in the glen where she waited patiently for Laylan. Nenamis once again waited at the edge of the clearing where he could observe Sarabie's lesson. The sky was a dull grey making the glen shadier than it would normally have been.

Laylan walked placidly into the glen and sat beside Sarabie. "Today I am going to explain to you the reason why you are here." Sarabie nodded in response and listened intently. "Long ago a war raged between, the elves, the dwarves, and the humans. At the very beginning all beings were the same; everyone was equal. Over time they strayed from their paths, and so developed the different races. Animals and dragons were given to us; a gift from the lord, to try and help us back on the correct track. We cherished this gift; for you see we still trusted the great lord, and made an ancient pact to remain faithful to him. The humans took dragons like Niver Nenamis, and killed them, only to make their feasts more grand, and their clothes more exuberant. They did; and still do not, think of dragons as living beings. The dwarves captured the dragons and forced them to be used as weapons; they ordered them to destroy other beings, which is not in the nature of a dragon. And so this is when the dragons fled. The three races fought amongst each other, people of our race were captured and tortured to death. We know very little of the dwarves, however, men we have managed to keep a close eye on. Your father has made a plan to destroy all other races except for his own. He thinks of us as dirty half bloods, he thinks us stupid and ignorant; this is because his mind is closed to all that surrounds him, he does not know the truth. What makes it harder for everyone is that humans do not care to know the truth; they believe that only their way is correct, and if anyone should stand to oppose their beliefs then they do not hesitated to kill. Of course you know this by the actions of your father, he killed your mother, and he tried to kill you. It is our mission as elves to stop the humans before they destroy the earth; you have seen how peaceful we elves are, and how simply and contently we live, we do not need grandeur, we have each other.

You however are very different; you are not dwarf, human, or elf. You are a gift from the lord.

We are praying that you are the one Sarabie, for the world's sake. You are more powerful than anyone could have guessed. Do you see what must be done?"

"We must show the humans their path, and those that cannot open their hearts will have to be killed, a war will rage; but the elves will win."

"Yes; hard as it is it must be done. You can see how they are destroying the earth. What your father did to you is unacceptable; however thousands of other people suffer the same torture. We must put a stop to this!" There was a silence that filled the ill lit glen, it hovered for a moment but was then broken by Sarabie. "I must kill my father."

"I believe that perhaps it is one step on a long journey."

"I will do it."

"You must receive more training first; learn about the finer arts of battle, then you will be ready."

Sarabie smiled weakly and turned to face Laylan. "It maybe one of the hardest things I have to do, but it must be done for the good of the Earth." She shifted closer to the elf. "You have been very kind to me Laylan."

"I have done what I promised your mother." Sarabie gazed up at the dull sky and thought silently to herself. "I feel that I am ready to take on the world, magic comes naturally to me, I feel no drain of energy; and Nenamis said that should I ever run out of energy then I may use his. We have become so close; we no longer have to share thoughts, we can share emotions instead."

"Yes, your souls are joined; to sides of the same coin." Sarabie turned to face Laylan.

"I think sometimes that perhaps you and I are as well."

"What makes you think that?" Laylan leant towards Sarabie.

"We are similar in our ways; and perhaps share the same passions. Our paths are intertwined."

They looked in too each others eyes; they both moved towards each other, gaze fixed upon each others eyes. There lips met and they kissed passionately. Nenamis hummed quietly from the side of the glen, he silently bid farewell to Sarabie and walked into the depths of the forest.

• •

Sarabie awoke to find herself lying beside Laylan; he was still fast asleep. She rose and examined her surroundings. It was late into the evening and the clouds had cleared to reveal the bright stars glistening down upon them.

Nenamis where are you.

Not far. Sarabie followed the energy from within his conscience and found him sat beside a large tree stump. She leapt on to his back and settled herself between his tines.

Have fun did you?

Hmm; come on we're going on a journey.

Do I no where?

Err, yes I think you do, and with that the dragon leapt in to the air, brushing through the woodland canopy and out in to the open sky.

. . . .

Laylan crawled from the glen feeling ashamed. He did not understand his feelings towards Sarabie. Did he really sleep with her because he loved her, or because Carman had told him to gain her trust; or could it even have been that he had neglected his promises to himself and had fallen in to the hand of sin?

He walked into the snowdrop filled glen and sat beside a waiting Carman.

"You're late."

"I am sorry." He answered glumly.

"Well, has she gone?"

"Yes she has."

"Good, I'm glad you were able to gain her trust; it looks like we will be able to use her after all."

Laylan looked sadly at Carman, a tear trickling slowly down his face. His heart seemed to be beating slower than usual and his body became numb as a curtain of regret and depression swept over him.

I can't believe I let this happen.

CHAPTER 14

The Foundations Of A War

"And so it was that man was destroyed and the world found peace."

DEAN RODE AHEAD of his army, he chose not to look at them, or the mass of prisoners they had. Weary looking men rode worn down horses. The beasts staggered and stumbled as they made their way over the rocky ground; the men struggled to keep their eyes open, and they slouched heavily in their saddles. Following the army, chained to the horses, were dying women and children; also with them were stray dwarves and elves. There legs were weak and broken, their feet smashed and bleeding; and those unable to still walk on their shattered limbs were dragged along the floor by chains around their necks. All of the prisoner's wrists and ankles were chained together, restricting their movement; sores covered the areas bounds by chains, the metal links digging into their flesh until there was none left, only bone. The children screamed and cried out as their parents were tortured to death. The children then would suffer the same painful end.

The army now consisted of ten thousand men, the entire kingdom had been raided and they were now on the march back to Karbith's castle. Rain poured down upon their bloody faces, filth muddying their garments. Fear kept the soldiers going, they thought only of their families; the sooner the war ended, the sooner they could return to their loved ones back home. They pictured what would happen should they refuse to fight; their families would face the same fate as the prisoners that they themselves were torturing.

Tarlin, Kaylin's head of defense, rode amongst the army. Tears rolled steadily down his face; he saw the people around him suffering, he felt ashamed that he was too much of a coward to do something to help them. However he then thought to himself that he now had nothing to loose, his family was already dead, and he cared little for anyone, so why should he sit here and watch innocent people being tortured when he could help them. But then many of the injured wouldn't make it anywhere, they would all die in the process of running away, some appeared too far gone now to be saved. Tarlin needed to think, how could he save as many people as possible, and perhaps even stop Dean; then if he stopped Dean, what about Karbith, who was there strong enough to defeat him?

. . . .

Tarlin offered to stand guard for the evening, with a few of his fellow comrades who used to work with him for Kaylin. They sat around the fire and discussed Tarlin's thoughts from earlier on in the day.

"We must do something; we can not sit back and watch as this kingdom is destroyed."

"No Tarlin we can not. Do you have a plan?" a stout man with a rough beard that covered most of his face said this; his name was Firmus.

"We must leave the army, run into the foot hills of Bulagger Mountain. We must seek the dwarves, perhaps they will help us; I believe they are our only hope." The men surrounding Tarlin all looked shocked. "Tarlin we cannot do that, have you not heard what lies in that mountainous range?"

"Yes Ignus, I have. However I think that our fate here would be worse than our fate in the foothills of Bulagger." There were a few nods and mumbles of agreement,

"You are right Tarlin, I will follow you." Firmus looked round at the other men. They gazed back at him, deciding their fate. "I too will follow you Tarlin." This time a tall gangly man stood up and clenched his fists, "They have killed all my family, I don't want them to kill any one else's." Tarlin smiled and nodded at the man, "Thank you, Gandis."

One by one the other men in the group began to nod their agreement, however there were two men sat to the edge of the group. They communicated with each other silently, before rising, and crept away silently, unnoticed.

"When will we leave Tarlin?" asked Gandis. Tarlin thought for a moment,

"Why not now, there are no other guards about, they would not notice until morning, and by then we would be long gone." The men surrounding Tarlin gazed at him with admiration, they valued his bravery.

"Well I will gather supplies," offered Firmus.

"No, we must travel light, anyway there are little supplies left; once we reach the hills we will be able to hunt for food. Until then we will have to bare our hunger." Once again the men nodded in agreement. "Right we must gather horses. We must meet by the Oak tree just to the west of camp. You all have ten minutes" Tarlin did a quick head count and counted seventeen men. They dispersed and Tarlin left to tack up his horse. "We are leaving Spirit, we must find help." The stallion snorted in response. The horse was a stunning black, his mane flowed down his shoulder, and his neck arched high as the saddle was placed upon his back. Once the bridle was fitted, Tarlin mounted and trotted out of the small paddock created of stakes and rope, and saw in many directions, his fellow men doing the same.

They all met at the oak tree, Tarlin counted sixteen riders, "Where is Firmus?"

"Did he not go to get supplies?" replied Gandis.

"No he didn't, I told him we were to travel light." Tarlin rapidly took in the view of the camp. He saw lights moving amongst the small canvas tents. "Ride!!" Tarlin spurred Spirit into a gallop, the horse leapt forward with no hesitation. The horses grouped together with fear, their eyes rolls and their nostrils flared as arrows came flying towards them. The men leant forward over their horses necks and urged them on, praying that lady luck would be with them.

They saw before them the ground rising; they pushed the horses up the hill and dropped down the bank on the other side. "Quick, the wood!" Tarlin led the group right towards the forest; they now galloped along the bottom of the hill. The ground shook under the horses hooves, the air misted with their breath. Upon the other side of the hill, the men could hear half of Karbith's army galloping towards them. This only encouraged them to push their horses harder; this was a race for their lives. The cover of the tree's grew nearer, the sound of pounding hooves also grew louder; they could now hear the men's shout over the brow of the hill.

With one last push the horses leapt through the undergrowth and landed exhausted into the forest. Tarlin pulled Spirit to a halt and spun him around to look out across the hill beside them. Through the dark, he could see a hundred or so men galloping down the hillside and across the open plain.

Due to the lack of light, it was hard to see into the forest, therefore Karbith's army failed to see Tarlin, so galloped onward.

Tarlin let out a sigh of relief. "Well done men. It is apparent that Firmus betrayed us. We must keep riding; we will keep to a trot, and continue through the forest, I fear that to ride directly along the plain maybe too dangerous, so for now we will stick to the cover of the trees."

The men surrounding Tarlin nodded and took in his words, although some did look deathly white. So it was then that Tarlin and his small army of sixteen men rode through the moonlit forest, in search of freedom.

. . . .

However back at the camp Firmus was doing the opposite of what Tarlin had thought he was doing. Firmus was chained to a pole and was covered in deep slashes that spilt blood upon the now deep red grass. He was surrounded by five or so men, two of them being the ones that had overheard Tarlin previously and one being of course Dean himself.

"What are they planning to do?" Dean demanded as a burley man held a blade to Firmus's throat.

"I've already told you, I don't know." Firmus's face was hard and cold, and no emotion seemed to be behind his dark brown eyes. "Even if I did know, I would never tell you."

The chains in which were tied around his ankles and wrists had been drawn so tightly that the joints had now begun to bleed. A vivid slash was upon his rugged face making the man seem more sinister than he really was. No matter what torture the men around him inflicted, Firmus would never be fazed, for inside he felt more pain than any physical wound. Every day it felt to him as though his heart had been ripped in two, and every day his heart bled.

"Just kill me." Firmus said simply, for deep inside that was his biggest wish; for this living nightmare to be over. His hope was that when he died he would go to a better place, and he would finally see his wife and children again. However he did not mind if this were not true, for within his mind he felt that to be dead would be better than to be here.

Dean nodded to the guard stood closest to Firmus; and with one quick flick of is sword; the guard removed Firmus's head.

The guards walked away and left the body chained to the post. Firmus's heart had stopped, and with it the pain.

CHAPTER 15

Agractabeo

*"A land that is lost bears many secrets that are perhaps better
left uncovered. For many things are lost, because they are not
meant to be found."*

Rose and Laylan were flying towards a large mountain range, as
the light began to dim Thalayli landed in the heart of a grassy
valley. The valley walls rose up around them offering them protection
from the elements. The bright sun shone upon the horizon, leaving the
sky a pale shade of pink. Laylan and Rose dismounted and sat upon
the grass.

*I must eat, I will go and hunt; I will bring you both back a portion of what
ever I catch.* And with that the mighty dragon took flight again, leaving
the girl and the elf alone in the green valley.

"I am glad he has healed so well," said Laylan, his hair rippling in
the wind.

"He has not healed, at all."

"What do you mean?"

"He has lost something, I don't know what it is, he's just not right."
Laylan thought to himself, he could not understand what Rose was
saying, however he chose not to question.

"Is there anything you can do about it?"

"Well probably if I knew what it bloody was," Rose turned away so as not to face the elf, there was a pause. "I am hiding from him, and I know it has put a wall between us, but there is nothing I can do."

"Why is it so important not to tell him?" Laylan took a small step towards Rose. "I want to help you Rose."

"You can not help me any more Laylan. I can not be helped by any one; I am in over my head."

"And there is no way for you to be helped? You know Rose there are many people who would help you."

"Who you and Thalayli, an elf and a dragon . . . ."

"The two most powerful beings on this earth."

"Yes, and they still aren't powerful enough, perhaps this is just the way It must be." Laylan shook his head and continued to gaze at Rose. "I just wish to help."

Rose did not answer. She sat down upon the grass still facing away from the elf. He spun around and looked out across the valley. "Rose did you hear that?" he turned to face her and saw that she had already drawn her sword and was staring in the same direction that he had been looking. Rose strode forward to stand beside the elf, and both of them with swords drawn faced the brow of the hill.

The sound of thundering hooves grew nearer; shouts also were deciphered within the noise. After a few minutes horses were visible, they galloped flat out down the side of the valley, heading straight towards Rose and Laylan. Men dressed in travel worn army uniform sat astride tired looking horses. The animals panted heavily, and as they were brought to a halt in front of the girl and the boy, their sides heaved and sweat dripped from their glistening bodies.

"Who are you and what is your business?" demanded one of the leading officers.

"My name is Gregory and this is my wife Perdi, our business is our own."

"Not any more it isn't why are you so heavily armed?"

"We had heard that thieves walked these valleys," Laylan glanced quickly at Rose and noted that she wore a snarl and appeared ready to fight should the worst happen. A soldier from the back of the ride rode forward. "That's an elf."

"Seize them!" shouted the commanding officer. The troops moved forward to surround Laylan and Rose. Four of the men leapt from their steeds and approached; Laylan had to do very little as Rose had leapt forward and left the four soldiers laid dead and bleeding upon the grass.

Laylan gawped at Rose, "It would seem that your skill has improved over the years." Rose grinned and turned to face the soldiers, "Anymore for anymore?" she growled at them.

This time ten soldiers burst forward and ten archers showered her with arrows. Rose reflected the arrows with a quick flick of her wrist; she moved at the speed of light as she deflected blows from the soldier's swords, she then leapt into the air, knees bent; she then seemed to push the air down with her hands; as she did this a green light emitted from her palms; it soared downwards towards the soldiers standing beneath her. The light hit the ground causing the entire earth to shake; the men were thrown from the ground, they then landed in all directions, mangled and broken they hit the earth dead. Only the man that had spoken first still sat astride his horse alive. He looked around at his fallen comrades, "What are you?" he snarled.

"I am what I am." Rose smirked and turned to Laylan, "What do you want me to do with this one?"

Laylan stood for a moment gazing at the thirty or so men that lay dead around him.

"Why were you hunting us? What is going on with Karbith?" asked Laylan.

"It is none of your business." snapped the man.

"I think it is my business when you are intending to capture me."

"You were to be captured and taken to the king for questioning." The soldier said this rapidly, as though saying it faster would make it easier, and less of a betrayal to his king.

"And what does the king intend to find out from questioning me?" The soldier remained silent; however Rose saw him look quickly at the valley before them as though planning his escape. So she leapt towards him, sword in hand, and drew the blade to his throat.

"Easy, easy," said the man. The blade was pressed to his throat hard enough to draw blood.

"The king wants to know where Elvendin is hidden." The man was shaking as this tumbled from his mouth.

Laylan nodded to Rose and she slit the mans throat; his body went limp and he fell from his horse to the ground, where he lay dead beside his fellow warriors.

"Well, it is now obvious that Karbith doesn't know the whereabouts' of Elvendin." Laylan said as he turned to face a blood covered Rose.

"Oh, I think he does."

"What makes you think that?"

"Because they weren't trying very hard to capture us, in fact they were more or less trying to kill us."

Laylan sighed and examined his feet. "Perhaps you are right, it is my worst thought confirmed."

Rose turned to look up at the sky, "Thalayli is returning, he has food."

With that comment Laylan saw a red and black dragon soar over the horizon. He approached them rapidly, and soon had landed beside them; a deer hanging limp in his mouth.

He placed the carcass on the floor and gazed at the mass of bodies surrounding them.

I could hear death on the wind and assumed that you two would be the source of it.

Rose smiled and nodded.

An hour or so later, the trio were well fed and nestled themselves down to rest for the evening.

"Rose may I ask were you gained such power?" asked Laylan as they sat beside a warm, golden fire. "And also I do not understand how you do not suffer any more. I mean when . . . well lets just say before you disappeared you were in complete turmoil, what happened?"

"You may ask but I will not answer." Rose said this as she avoided the elf's gaze, as though some how he may be able to look in to her face and see the truth.

Laylan sighed and turned to look at Thalayli. The dragon shook his head slightly and twisted his head round to rest it under his wing as he readied to sleep.

"What is it Rose? What has changed you?"

"It does not concern you." Rose got up and walked over to Thalayli where she rested herself beside him and nestled under his wing beside his head.

Laylan remained deep in thought for a few moments before he too rose and settled himself on Thalayli's other side.

. . . .

Thalayli's sleep that night was restless; he saw before him a great battle. There appeared to be three armies fighting in the war, the murders were brutal and the plains were covered in a sea of blood. The battle raged, though over the horizon approached another army. They were all powerful; they used magic and had soon killed all of the other armies. They began to turn on each other, tearing each other apart. These beings had grand wings of different colors, covered in feathers similar to those of swans. Were these creatures angels? Apart from their wings they appeared human, yet they could use magic. The earth was soon destroyed, nothing was left, just an ocean of death.

Thalayli opened his eyes; he had not been dreaming, it was a vision. He seemed completely aware of his surroundings; he could hear Laylan and Rose as they breathed heavily in their sleep. The moon was still high in the sky, and the stars winked at the large dragon.

If I have just seen the future, he thought to himself; *then we are all doomed.* He shook his head gently and returned to sleep.

. . . .

And you're sure this wasn't just a dream? Asked Rose in the morning.

I am no idiot Rose. Thalayli described to Rose in great detail his vision from the previous night.

You've gone bloody mad dragon.

Don't say that, I believe what I saw. Rose shrugged and ended the conversation.

"It is about a three hour fly from here." Rose said as she mounted Thalayli. Laylan nodded, "May I ask how you know where the dwarves are hiding?"

"Well I had to go somewhere when I was exiled by you elves."

Laylan sighed and answered, "Yes I suppose so, what did you find there?"

"Exile."

"Oh, and are you not worried about the dwarves killing you when you walk through their doors? Do you not expect the same thing to happen that happened in Elvendin?"

"Mmm yes, but I can handle axes and swords, however when fifty odd spells are thrown at you, it is pretty hard to send them away from you."

"I see your point." With that Laylan leapt on to Thalayli's back, where he nestled himself behind Rose.

With one effortful leap Thalayli leapt into the sky, beating the air with his tremendous wings.

Hours they flew upon the ocean of air, Thalayli's beating wings never failing from their steady rhythm. The wind stung their faces as they began to descend through the air. As Thalayli brought his wings to their full extension, their descent began to slow, and rather heavily, they hit the ground; sending the elf and the girl lurching forwards up his neck.

The trio had landed beside a large grey mound that stood at around twenty feet tall. Its surface was rough and had many foot holes in it that were noticeably used for steps.

"Ab Rose, debirio revisi dath commeneo adoris." Rose spoke, clearly. Laylan looked at the girl quizzically. "I did spend almost a year with them." She said, answering his gaze.

"Adoris curi accipio despergo." From upon the top of the mound rose a pint sized being, he was all off three feet tall, had a great beard of brown coarse hair that was neatly tucked in to a green scaled belt. An axe was held in one of his stubby hands, and a small broad sword was hung across his back. The dwarf growled and leapt; and with one rapid movement, he landed heavily on the ground in front of them with a dull thud.

"What are you doing hear, Atrus Cordis?" snarled the stocky dwarf.

"As I said before, I have come to warn you?" Rose said this perfectly calmly, and took a step towards the dwarf.

"And I am to believe that am I?"

"Well yes you are?"

"After all the lies you told us in the past; all the things you did?" The dwarf spat at Rose's feet.

"I did those things for a reason."

"So you think what you did was acceptable?" The dwarf's voice was now barely audible, as he growled this.

"I had no choice."

"So you stick to your reasons; we thought you were under our command, then find out you were under another's; how can we trust you?"

"You cannot, however this warning is of upmost importance, the humans are rallying and intend to wipe out your race." The dwarf took a step back and took in the trio.

"How do you know this?"

"Because Karbith told me."

"And you trust him?"

"That is just it, I don't trust him. I am warning you because you still have a place on this earth, you deserve to fight for your freedom; not just have it snatched from you whilst you are sleeping in your beds."

"How do I know that this isn't just some ploy to create war within the kingdom?"

"If I wanted a war to be brought about then I could cause it myself; I believe that there are enough people out there that want me dead to create an army." The dwarf considered this for a moment.

"Come in," the dwarf turned to face the boulder then whispered, "Karkarith." The surface of the boulder directly in front of them seemed to dissolve leaving a gapping hole. A tunnel appeared that seemed to lead into the centre of the earth.

I shall wait for you here, said Thalayli from within Rose's mind. She nodded in acknowledgement and strode into the mist of the boulder; the elf and the dwarf followed.

"Bit dark in here isn't it." Said Laylan. The dwarf glowered at him and continued to waddle down the tunnel. They were surrounded by pitch black, and were unable to even see their hands in front of their faces. However it only seemed to be Laylan that struggled with the lack of vision. He reached out to Rose with his mind, *how on earth am I meant to see where we are going?*

Reach out with your mind, feel your surroundings with your conscious; and remember you will find light in even the darkest of places.

Laylan reached out with his mind and found the walls of the tunnel, he then realized he had his eyes closed; he opened them and saw right to the far end of the tunnel. It glowed white and it appeared to be the ray of light that gave Laylan the hope that the tunnel would end.

Soon enough the tunnel opened out and they were stood in what looked like a large entrance hall; many doors led off from the hall. The dwarf walked straight ahead through the largest of the doors. They were now in yet another tunnel and Laylan was beginning to feel quite claustrophobic.

Therefore it wasn't long before he passed out; however Rose and the dwarf continued down the tunnel, not having noticed that Laylan was unconscious on the floor.

Rose and the dwarf had now reached a well lit cavern. Jewels glittered from the walls and the ceiling, all of them different colors, and they shone a rainbow of light down upon the ground.

"If you wait here a moment I will ask for an audience with the king." The dwarf tottered off through another passage to the left of the cavern.

Rose paced the cavern deep in thought; she still had not noticed Laylan's absence. She then stood in the centre of the cavern admiring the jewels.

"When I was first here this cavern contained no jewels. When I was exiled they placed a jewel in the wall for every person I killed." The hundreds of jewels glistened down at her. When no answer came to her she looked round in search for the elf. "Oh bollocks."

. . . .

Laylan awoke to find himself still sat alone in the tunnel. He felt the ground rumbling beneath him; he sat up, his head still feeling fuzzy, and heard foot steps coming rapidly towards him. He rose quickly and hid behind a boulder to his right. He could hear grumbling voices.

"Yes Groth, she is here; hence why our immediate presence is required." The dwarf spoke in a deep husky voice. Laylan could see nothing in the darkness, but guessed that there were around forty dwarves marching down the tunnel.

"Why is she here, she was banished?"

"We should have just killed her when we had the chance" came a third voice.

"Do you not remember?" growled a forth, even deeper voice. "We tried, stabbed her through the heart."

"Are you saying that she's immortal?" This was said by the second voice.

"Well she ain't really got a heart to stab has she?" There was a hearty laugh from the dwarves.

"Now let's get going, no one can live if they ain't got a head can they?" An even heartier, bellowing laughter followed this.

"Oh shit," whispered Laylan.

. . . .

Rose stood in the gemmed cavern twiddling her thumbs; she was growing rather bored.

"Ah, Madam Rose; it's so err pleasant to see you again." A well dressed dwarf strode up to her and offered her his hand. She shook it briefly as she didn't want to hurt her back from bending down to much. He then turned and shuffled to the end of the cavern, "please, follow me." Rose did as she was told, and walked steadily behind the dwarf. The pair then entered a small room with high stone walls. At the far end sat the tiniest of all dwarves, no more then two feet tall. His beard and hair was plaited, and he wore rich golden robes with a heavy golden belt which did nothing to contain the dwarf's over large belly as it escaped from over the top of the belt making it only half visible.

The dwarf did not get up from his throne, probably because of the fear of having to go through the embarrassment of having to be lifted back on to it.

"Why are you here, Atrus Cordis?" the dwarf spoke in an incredibly high pitched voice, so high in fact that dogs the other side of the kingdom could have heard him.

"I have come to warn you; however, have any of your men come across an elf, he was with me and now he seems to have just gone poof?"

"No we have not; you there send a scout to search for the elf." A dwarf stood next to the tunnel to the cavern nodded and scurried off in to the darkness. "What do you know of Karbith?"

"He has raised an army, and a large one; he made it compulsory for all men to join."

The dwarf spat on the dry earth beside him, "how do you know this, last time I heard you were not his ally."

"I was present when he killed Kaylin, we then fought; and he told me of his plans."

"Willingly?"

"Yes, but do not forget that I am no fool. Karbith was boasting to me of his new learnt skill in magic, for no other reason did he bring me there than to test his strength; the boy longs for revenge."

"And what did you do to upset him, kill the wrong person?"

"Yes actually, I did."

"You are a fool Atrus Cordis."

"No I think you misheard me, I just said that I am not a fool."

"Really?" as the dwarf lord said this a hundred dwarves seemed to step out from the darkness that surrounded the far walls of the large room.

"You are a fool to think that you can just walk in here, and leave alive." The dwarves approached her, their eyes mad with anger. "After what you did to us, how can you expect us to trust you? We want you dead; you have taken many of our families, and what for? No, you won't even explain yourself."

"The day draws nearer when you will understand." The dwarf king roared and the army of dwarves charged. Rose sighed and vanished.

"What the . . . . ?" the king gazed around trying to figure out where she had gone.

"Behind you mate." The small dwarf spun round and saw Rose stood calmly behind him. The king toppled heftily off his throne and landed in a mass of gold cloth on the floor.

The dwarf army charged towards Rose, not having noticed the king in a heap on the ground. He was quickly trampled as they rushed at Rose, all of them wanting their share of her blood. They were within a foot of her when she vanished again, this time she reappeared by the entrance back to the cavern.

"Rose!"

"Laylan, where the hell have you been?"

"Fainted, claustrophobic; just thought that I would let you know that the dwarves are plotting to kill you."

"Bit late for that don't you think, now go bird!" With that Rose transformed in to a wolf. It took Laylan a while to understand what she had said; he then leapt in to the air and morphed in to an eagle. He swooped low over Rose and followed her back through the cavern, back in to the tunnel and in to the entrance hall.

Which door, asked Laylan.

Er let me think, the one we came in through perhaps.

Sarcasm is the lowest form of wit.

I had no intention of being witty.

The bird and the wolf approached the door directly in front of them; with tremendous skill Rose opened the door with her teeth and galloped down the dark tunnel. Laylan flew above her; they travelled for only a few moments before Laylan flew straight in to the wall at the end of the tunnel. He slid down the wall and landed in a crumpled heap on the ground.

There's a wall there, said Rose, baring her teeth in a wolfish grin.

You don't say, croaked Laylan.

Rose changed back in to human form and whispered, "Karkarith." The entrance to the outside world appeared, and the pair stepped out in to the glorious sunshine.

About time, said Thalayli as they approached him.

Sorry, kind of got attacked.

What do you mean kind of?

Rose showed him the memory of their attack. The dragon rumbled from deep down in his soul. *I expected as much.*

The trio then flew a few leagues south and made camp for the night. Rose stood up and stretched, "Rose wait," Laylan walked swiftly up to her, he had his hand clasped firmly on the hilt of his sword.

"Yes Laylan," quick as a flash the elf drew his sword and forced it straight through her stomach and out the other side.

Rose glared at him, "What the hell was that in aid off."

"It's funny you know, people generally scream in pain when a sword has been driven through them."

"Sorry, I'll remember that in future." She stepped back and the blade slid from her torso. Black fluid gushed from the wound; Laylan looked on quizzically as she healed the gash in her stomach.

"Was that blood?"

"Yes why?"

"Since when was blood black?" once again Rose glared at him.

"It is none of your business what ruddy color my blood is."

"Why can't you die?"

"What?"

"You heard."

"Like you said before, I went to hell and got kicked straight back out again." Laylan looked at her, as though seeing her for the first time. He said no more, just walked round to Thalayli's furthest side and settled for sleep.

As Rose lay beside the dragon, curled up under his wing, she felt alone; she felt as though her existence was completely insignificant and pointless.

· ·

Rose could not sleep, she dozed on and off; bored of this, she got up and walked away from the other two who were snoring very annoyingly. She walked for a while, then sat and watched the night pass by. She relaxed into the night and reached her mind out to everything around her.

"About time I saw you again." Rose did not turn to face the person to whom she had addressed; instead she chose to continue to gaze at the distant horizon.

"Beginning to look forward to my visits are you?"

"Not at all," Rose snarled.

"Now, now, no need to get hurtful."

"I'll do as I bloody well like." Rose ground her teeth, then spat.

"Ughk, dirty habit spitting." A tall figure stepped in front of Rose. He wore a long black cloak, his hair was a dark brown, and his eyes a dark green. He had an angular face with sharp features; he seemed to radiate a sense of superiority.

"I want you to go somewhere for me." Rose turned away from the young man and gazed at the sky.

"Where?"

"Agractabeo." Rose shook her head. The man took a step closer to her; they were now only a foot apart.

"I want to train you, make you stronger. Then your work will be complete quicker and you will be free."

"What other training can I receive?" Rose looked briefly in to the mans eyes, and then quickly looked away.

"Oh, there are a lot of things you don't yet know, I will teach you the ways of energy itself; how to control things without using an ounce of energy." Rose listened intently.

"You will be more powerful than the great creator himself. It's all there for the taking." He crouched down towards her, "I am here for you, I can see your potential; your true self. You can see that now surely." Rose grabbed the man by the scruff of his cloak and pulled them both upright.

"What is the purpose of this war?" she growled at him, her face only inches from his.

"Why, to bring peace of course. Can the elves and the dwarves really spend the rest of eternity hidden away?"

"What's in it for you?"

"Well I suppose I will have a few more comrades, but other wise nothing. You always seem to think the worst of me."

"Can you blame me considering who you are?"

"No I suppose not, though I must admit that this is a very lonely job." The man grinned and moved even closer to Rose. She however stepped away and looked out across the plain to the side of her.

"Oh, come on; don't tell me you didn't enjoy it last time?" The smirk upon his face grew wider and he walked towards Rose. He ran his hand through her hair; she turned to face away from him. He then ran his finger down her cheek, then across the scar upon her eye. He looked down at her charmingly. She looked up in to his eyes and lost herself. This time she did not turn away, she welcomed his contact, his embrace; and together they chased away the night.

· ·

"Where on earth have you been?" yelled Laylan as Rose walked back in to camp, late the following morning.

"I went for a walk."

"What through a bush? Look at the state of you, you're a mess." Rose rolled her eyes and attempted to flatten her hair and brush the mud of her garments.

Where did you go last night? Asked Thalayli,

Like I said I went for a walk.

"I'm going to Agractabeo."

"What! Why?" said Laylan, a little hysterically.

"I must."

"Oh, god; not this again?"

"Yes again. I am going this afternoon, don't try to stop me."

"You are aware of what the name Agractabeo means don't you, it means land of devils. Why would you want to go to a place like that?"

"I am fully aware of the kind of place it is however it is there in which I must go."

"Then I will let you, but know that I am not coming with you."

"That's fine, but what will you do?"

"I err . . . ." Laylan thought for a moment, "I'm not sure yet."

"Ok, well whilst you make up your mind, I'll remove evidence of camp, yes? Then when it is time to leave you may give me your answer." Rose put out the fire with a swift movement of her hand, and she burned all traces of food.

"Decided yet?"

"I'm coming with you."

"What?"

"You heard."

"Very well." With that the girl, the elf, and the dragon took to the skies once more.

Chapter 16

A Journey For Jack

*"When the end of the world is nigh, will you embrace it,
or run and hide?"*

JACK WALKED ALONG the beach searching for something that he knew of not. His feet sunk in the sand and he could hear shells being broken beneath his footsteps. He turned around and looked back across the beach; he saw two sets of footprints. He was now highly confused seeing as he only had one pair of feet so could only leave one set of footprints.

"Good afternoon Jack," came a smooth confident voice.

"You're late, I have been waiting all day; you said you would be here this morning." A sly grin crept across the mans face, his dark brown hair rippling in the sunlight.

"Yes I know, I was, shall we say, otherwise engaged." The grin grew wider and he tilted his head slightly; his long black cloak swaying with the soft breeze.

"Are you saying that you had a meeting more important than ours?"

"It was equally important as my meeting with you; however, this other appointment was, shall we say, a great deal more pleasurable." The man smirked then turned to continue walking down the beach.

"So what is it you wish me to do?" asked Jack.

"I want you to go to an island called, Agractabeo. It is not far from where we are stood. You must cross the vast expanse of water before us, and then you will reach the island. There you will be trained; you will be taught how to use your new power."

"Will this help me destroy Rose, Dean and Karbith?"

"Ah, slight technical hitch there when it comes to Rose."

"She deserves to die; she killed all those innocent people."

"Well you see Rose is on our side."

"What?"

"I believe you heard me?" The grin on the man's face had gone and he turned to face Jack. "Those people were killed because I ordered it, is that understood."

"Why? Why is she working for you?"

"The same reason as you, well a similar reason anyway." The man tilted his head slightly as though viewing the world from an angle allowed him to see it more clearly.

"She doesn't need any more power to fore fill any form of revenge," Jack retorted.

"It was not revenge she sought; it was life."

"Are you saying that you were the one who resurrected her?" There was a long silence which was broken when Jack fell down a hole in the sand. The man offered him no hand to help him up; he merely watched as Jack struggled to his feet.

"Who are you?"

"Like I have said before; I'm someone who can help. Now will you go to Agractabeo?"

"How will I cross the water?"

"I'm sure you can use your new found power to help you cross a small section of water?" Jack though about this for a moment.

"What do you expect me to do, walk on water?"

"That's exactly what I want you to do." And with that the man evaporated in to thin air leaving Jack completely alone.

"Oh, great; thanks for that." Jack sat down on the sand and gazed out across the sea. Far in the distance he saw a small dark shadow that he guessed was Agractabeo.

"So unhelpful." He pondered the water for a while; wondering how he could manipulate the water to hold his weight.

After many long hours, when the sky began to turn purple as the sun slowly sunk into the horizon, Jack rose and walked up to the waters edge. The tide washed in and out clawing at the earth. Jack reached out with his mind and felt the surface of the water. He stepped forward and felt the cold water underfoot. He felt with his conscience the pressure of the water, he pushed at it with his mind; it seemed to put up a resistance to him, as though it was repelling him. He stepped onto the surface of the water. It held his weight. He took another step forward, and another. Jack couldn't believe it, he was walking on water. His attention was lost and he dropped into the cold water.

"Bugger." He concentrated on the waters surface again, and climbed upwards back on to the waters surface. This time he focused on the water and continued; one foot in front of the other.

He did not know how long he walked for; he dared not sway his concentration from the water. He just continued, seemingly for forever, concentrating on the waters surface and the resistance that it seemed to put up against him. Not once did Jack look up from the water beneath him. Not once did he look up just to see how far he had left to go, he just continued, knowing that this would not last forever.

When Jack first set foot on the dark, shadowy island, the sky was a pitch black; the stars glistening down on him flooded the island with light. He collapsed on the sandy beach, welcoming the rest. He felt exhausted; his body submitted to sleep.

Jack awoke to find the sun high above him, he was completely alone on the beach; the sand was a bright gold and the ocean appeared a cool, welcoming, blue. He sat upright and took in his surroundings. Behind him was a dense rainforest; from within it came loud cries emitted from birds and other animals that hid themselves from the rest of the world. Jack rose and gazed at the forest; he then looked left and right across the beach. It seemed to him that there was no other way apart from to go in to the rainforest. And so it was that he put his best foot forward and strode in to the depths of the foreboding rainforest.

Jack was surrounded by dense greenery; he could see little in either direction, only trees, trees and more trees. He walked for what seemed like hours, until he came to a river. At the river he bent down and scooped up some of the cool, fresh, water. It appeared clear in his hands and he sipped gratefully at the cold liquid. He then appreciated how thirsty he had been, he lapped away at the water, not noticing the being stood across the river from him.

"Heh hem." Jack reacted quicker than he had ever reacted. He sent the water spilling down his front, and searched his surroundings for the source of the voice.

"Across the river idiot." Came the voice again; Jack looked forward and saw the strange being stood a few feet away from him. The creature appeared human apart from the fact that it had huge blue wings sprouting from its back.

"Were you talking to me?" asked Jack; the being looked around then answered,

"Well there's no one else around is there?" Jack looked around himself then said,

"No I suppose not."

"My name is Calicus; I am here to help you train yourself. I have been asked by the master to guide you and show you the way, will you follow me?"

"Yes Calicus, I will." With that Jack crossed the water and joined Calicus as he walked in to the forest.

It was now that Jack was closer to Calicus that he could see him more clearly. His face was different; it seemed harsher; it was then that Jack noticed the deep furrows in Calicus's forehead and the top of his nose. His eyes were a dark blue, and his teeth seemed more canine than human.

However, Jack continued to follow Calicus through the forest with out the faintest idea of where they were going.

Chapter 17

The Death Of The King

"When the demons rise, will the angels have enough support to stop them; or will our lack of faith destroy the world?"

SARABIE AND NENAMIS soared through the skies, the dragon drifted on the breeze allowing the wind to carry him. The sky was a murky grey, rain splattered the ground; fog misted over the land obscuring the world beneath them.

We are here, said Sarabie. Nenamis dived towards the ground; he was rapidly picking up speed as he shot like an arrow through the air. The ground was approaching quickly, and it wasn't long before Nenamis began to slow their descent by spreading his wings to their maximum width. The air was caught under the thin membrane of his wings like a parachute, and Nenamis gently lowered himself to the ground with a few hefty buffets from his wings.

The girl and the dragon were now stood beside a small valley, from where they were stood they could hear a great river; it was called the river Orvan. A large drop was to their left, and beneath it was the great river.

How do you know he will be here? Asked Nenamis.

I can sense him. Sarabie scanned the surrounding area with her mind, and sure enough she found Garston's conscience. He was approaching them from through the forest to their right. He was with a hunting party of around ten men. They rode magnificent hunt horses, and hounds yapped at their heels. They soon emerged from the wood and stopped dead at the sight of Sarabie and Nenamis. Some of the horses bolted, leaving their riders in a heap on the floor.

"Sarabie!" barked Garston.

"Father." Sarabie growled, anger and hate shone in her eyes. She then noticed that there was then perhaps a small flicker of fear in the eyes of her father. "Get her, dead or alive." Screamed Garston; the surrounding men drew swords from their sheaths and charged at Sarabie. Quick as a flash she attacked, there was no need of assistance from Nenamis for all ten hunts men lay dead on the ground.

"Very impressive, I see that those blasted elves have taught you a few new tricks. Not surprising that they only teach you moves of death." Sarabie growled again too angry even to speak.

"Going to kill your own father are you Sarabie?"

"You killed my mother."

"I killed her for a reason?"

"And why was that?"

"Because she was a half blood, she was dirty, she was an elf"

"What?"

"That's right, you heard me and understood. Your mother was sent to me by the elves. She brought that blasted dragon egg with her. The elves made a pact with me that would make peace between the humans and the elves. We agreed to allow each other to live in peace. They told me that the egg would hatch for the next heir to the throne, some one with great power. But then you were born, you were to be queen. But I longed for a son, you were not worthy of becoming ruler of the kingdom. You did not deserve the throne, or the dragon."

"So why kill my mother?"

"Because I found out that Karbith is not my son, that is why I killed her, along with the fact that she planned to let you escape to the elves; and what was I supposed to do, allow the elves to train you, poison you against everything that is good, so that you would go and kill your own father? No, I had no intention of letting that happen. Your mother fell pregnant and I assumed it was mine, but now I know the truth. Your mother was a dirty, filthy, slag and deserved to die."

With that Sarabie charged forward, blade in hand. Garston deflected
her blows with a flick of his own sword. Again Sarabie aimed a blow,
and again it was deflected. They were moving as fast as the speed of
light. Their feet moved in repetitive rhythm as they edged closer and
closer to the edge of the cliff; Sarabie gaining ground the whole time.

Sarabie eyed the edge of the cliff as they grew closer to it; her
attention moving very briefly from her father. However in that split
second of her not on her full form, Garston swung his blade neatly
over hers and brought it down across her face. The sword left a large
gash from just above her left eyebrow to just below her cheek bone.
Blood gushed from the wound; her eye was now closed and was slowly
beginning to swell. Sarabie growled then lunged at her father; her
attention now solely on him, she would not make the same mistake
again.

Garston fought for his life knowing that he was no match for
Sarabie. He edged closer and closer to the edge; with one last effort he
drew his blade across Sarabie's sending her sword across the edge of
the cliff. With one swift wrist movement Sarabie used magic to disarm
Garston; his ruby red sword hit the ground a few feet away.

"This is the end Garston." With that Sarabie sent a blue force
towards her father, the light hit him square in the chest sending him
toppling over the edge of the cliff and in to the cold abyss of water
below.

Sarabie turned to face Nenamis, she grinned however he did not
return the smile. The half elf, half human girl picked up the ruby
incrusted sword and admired it.

I think this technically belongs to me now.

Do you think there was any truth in what your father said?

I don't know, Sarabie's smirk vanished.

We need to discuss this with Laylan.

Why didn't Laylan say anything before?

I don't know. I think we need to speak to him; it is a matter of urgency.

It was at that moment that Sarabie first heard it. *Thump, thump,
thump.* The dull thumping in her head sounded like a chorus of drums,
thump, thump, thump. Constant, over and over again. Sarabie gripped her
head with both hands, clawing at her hair as if to pull out the retched
noise. Thump, thump, thump. Then along with the thumping, came
a most horrific pain in her chest. It felt to her as though someone

had delved their fist straight in to her chest and was tearing her apart from inside. *Thump, thump, thump.* Sarabie screamed; Nenamis tried to comfort her but she couldn't hear him because of the drums and the pain. The girl collapsed, fists still clenching her head.

After a long period of this, Sarabie gathered enough strength to mount the dragon. Carefully Nenamis took off. They flew over the Orvan River and saw Garston's body washed up on the river bank, however Sarabie now began to fear what this murder had done to her.

They turned in mid-air and headed back towards Elvendin.

CHAPTER 18

Splitting Of Ways

*"When I am with you the pain stops; when I am with you
I could live forever."*

Laylan, Rose and Thalayli soared through the air, they could smell the ocean; taste the salt on their lips. They had been flying now for three hours and the cold was beginning to bite at their faces. Laylan was dozing as he clung on to Rose's waist; she however did not tire, she continued to gaze down at the earth.

It was then that Rose noticed, people moving in the distance, hundreds, thousands of them.

Thalayli let me use your eyes. Thalayli allowed Rose in to his conscience; she could feel every muscle of the mighty dragon's body. She saw through his eyes, all of a sudden being able to see far in to the distance, the world appeared clearer, sharper. She could see clearly an army, some were astride horses, and others were on foot.

As they drew nearer she could make out people being dragged along behind the army; they were bloody and broken, some appeared very close to death. Amongst the captives were children, elves and a few dwarves; the elves were unable to move, their bodies too badly broken to fight any more; they were dragged through the earth, not feeling, not caring. It was as though their souls had left their bodies, and only an empty shell was left.

The warriors did not appear to be that much happier; it was apparent that they were no longer human; pain and hurt had eaten away at their existences leaving nothing. They showed no sign of acknowledging the screams that were emitted from their captives; they simply continued to stumble along, tired and on the verge of surrendering their lives to death.

Rose then decided to wake Laylan; she now felt it necessary for him to witness the torture of his race.

"Laylan, I think you need to see this." The elf jumped, as though not really aware that he had been asleep. "What?" Rose looked across the valley towards the over large mass of torture. Laylan followed her gaze, and then he saw. He stared across at the army, hardly daring to believe what he was seeing. Rose turned to face him, "I'm sorry." She looked tenderly at him, understanding how he felt, for the first time in a long while, she felt another persons emotions; she felt his pain, his anger, the bitterness that was eating away at his heart.

Laylan dropped his gaze and stared at Thalayli's back. "I must return to my people, I must do what I should have done a long time ago." With that he leapt of the dragons back and soared through the air, mid fall he turned in to an eagle and began his journey back to Elvendin.

Has he returned for good? Asked Thalayli.

I would like to believe he has, it is about time. I fear he has been hiding from his true identity for a long time.

Thalayli did not answer Rose, He continued to fly onwards, avoiding going directly over the army.

The sea grew closer as they soared through the air. It was then not long before the dragon landed upon the beach.

Are you sure this is what you want to do? Thalayli tried to look deep in to her soul but saw nothing there. She nodded in reply and gazed out across the vast expanse of water.

I will not be able to join you on the island. Said the dragon gravely, *I have been with you too long now my dear friend; I have no intention of leaving you, however if you go to that island I fear our bond will break and our paths may not cross again.*

This is something I must do.

Why?

Because I do not break promises.

Do you not remember the promise you made to me? You said that love will bind us for ever; we are part of each other, joined, and never will we leave each other; not even death shall part us.

I do remember that promise, I will never forget it; all the time I remember myself, I shall remember you.

Yet you are willing to go across to Agractabeo, and break that promise.

I will never break that promise, hell did not break us and nor will this island, that is a promise.

Thalayli gazed at Rose, *I will hold you to that* promise, *I only hope that you stay true to yourself.*

The dragon turned and walked away, his head hung low; he knew that a great hope rested on Rose, only she did not know it; perhaps Rose's weight was even bigger than Sarabie's.

Rose watched the dragon depart, a black tear streaked down her face; she felt emotion.

She took a deep breath and pushed the thought of emotion aside as though it had never been there. Just as Jack had done, Rose stepped on to the water; she found it far easier to walk upon the waters surface than Jack, she strode forward purposefully and was soon stood on the beach on the island of Agractabeo.

She was greeted immediately by five winged beings. "Oh great, Aquilcornilus; just the creatures I wanted to see."

"Now, now Rose; we are not here to torture you this time. No we are here to help you." One of the creatures stepped forward; he had long black hair that matched his black wings.

"It's funny you know, I really don't trust you."

"Then perhaps you will learn. We are the teachers; not the punishers, you will find that our souls are lighter than that of our brothers down in hell. You will soon find your place here." The Aquilcornilus gestured in to the forest with his hand and inclined his head. "Will you follow us?"

Rose rolled her eyes, sighed then stepped in to the forest, flanked by the other winged beings.

CHAPTER 19

The Army Progresses

*"If the past is in the past, then how come it causes so
many problems in the future?"*

THE CASTLE WAS now in sight; it stood high upon a steep hill,
surrounded by a small town. Farms then sat at the bottom of
the hill, scattered about the countryside. Dean led his army and their
captives through the outskirts of the farms and headed straight in to
the heart of the town. As they stood at the entrance of the town,
looking up at its dark black gates, Dean turned to face his army.

"Men," he cried. "Only a select few of you will accompany me
in to the castle." He then pointed at five men stood to his left and
they then strode towards him to stand by his side. Dean nodded then
saluted the rest of the army; with that he opened the black gates and
led his horse and his guards in to the town.

As he remounted the grey mare and rode down the cobbled streets,
people gazed on with wary expressions. Dean made haste, avoiding
making eye contact with any of the peasants. Therefore it was not
long before they reached the small square courtyard at the front of the
castle. A footman stood at the entrance of the castle, he acknowledged
their presence and opened the grand oak door to allow them passage.
"If you will wait in the entrance hall sire, then I will proceed to alert

the king of your occupancy." Dean nodded to the door man, and then proceeded to examine the decor of the entrance hall. The walls were made of black and white marble, the ceiling and the floor consisted of the same smooth stone. A grand staircase led to the upper floor, its banister was constructed of serpents made from solid gold; the snakes twisted around each other.

It was only a few minutes before Karbith strode down the marble staircase. He threw out his arms and embraced Dean roughly, "You have done well, I see that you have gathered a very good army. You must rest, so must the army. Gather all of your strength, because you have a hard battle ahead. Rose has done just what I thought she would; the dwarves and the elves have been alerted. I will send a select few from the army to attack the creatures and hopefully draw them out of hiding; then a war shall rage." Karbith growled deep from within his throat.

"Yes, your majesty. Would you like for me to choose the ones who shall go to the elves and the dwarves?"

"No, I shall do it. I will give them magical protection. Now go, I will have the doorman take you to your quarters; when the time comes I will send for you, I will give you instructions and battle plans for the upcoming war. I will look in to having the soldiers skills perfected; when I have finished with your men you will not recognise them. Prepare yourself Dean, this is not a battle to be lost: Is that understood?"

"Yes sire, I understand. Thank you." Karbith then nodded, a sign that meant that Dean was free to leave. Dean turned and left the castle flanked by his five men.

Karbith waited until Dean was absent from the castle, before he strode back upstairs. The landing consisted of the same decor as the entrance hall. He entered a room that appeared to be a study. The walls were lined with hundreds of old tattered books that were thick with dust. He sat at a small wooden desk and examined a map that was laid out upon its surface. It was an old map, the parchment was an off yellowy brown. The map clearly showed the fine details of the kingdom; etched at the top right hand corner of the map was written; Regtrum ti fer derkus. Underneath this, written in what was obviously newer ink was; Kingdom of the Lord. Along the left hand side of the map had another series of words; Actlem orath hith pergon isthan orfathen terith iso candra. Next to this were more words scribbled in a different ink. These said; savior, power the lord knows not, dragon, belonging land. To anyone else these words and notes made little sense, however to Karbith they made all the sense in the world. A book was set beside the map; it was open on a page titled, Ce Libera et Viscis. But although he sat for hours gazing at the open book it still seemed to make little sense.

He had gained the book from a young elven child of no older than ten. It had appeared a bargain to the child to have swapped the book for a small piece of man made jewellery. The child was transfixed by the small bracelet that had belonged to Karbith's sister. However the child had been unaware that the book in which she had taken from her parents study, was in fact an ancient manuscript. It contained all the laws that were laid down by the great creator when the elves first chose to remain on the earth. The elf's parents were not very amused by the loss of the ancient manuscript, and it was not long before they were punished by the elven queen for its absence.

However, Karbith had known of the importance of the book; since he had entered Elvendin it had been his plan to steal it; he did not know however that it would be so easy. After all the planning he had done, the days of drawing out diagrams and studying the movements of those elves that kept the book. It had never occurred to him, and why should it, that the child would walk out of the house with it.

So Karbith was now sat over the book trying to decipher its meanings. He had found out that the majority of the book contained the tale of how the earth had been created; it also told of euphoria and hell. But what the king wanted to know most of all was what the section of the book that told of the prophecy meant. Karbith saw how close Rose and Thalayli were to the prophecy; he wanted to know how it was going to affect his plans. He wanted to know what power she would have, why was she so special? What made her different? This is what Karbith longed to know, he wanted answers; it was perhaps an obsession. However even after all of his patience in observation and cunning, he had still failed to decipher the messages laid within the book.

Since the creation of the great army, Karbith had done very little except dwell on the contents of the prophecy; this had totaled almost three whole months. After all this time Karbith had gained nothing, not even a fraction of understanding. What was this dark power? Touched by evil? It all sounded like codswallop to him.

After a further four hours of staring at the scripts in front of him, Karbith chose to retire. He left the study in the same condition as it had been in when he had entered it; a mess. He glanced back at the mass of books and parchments for one last time before heading of to his bed chamber.

Karbith lay awake for hours; how was Rose so significant that she was in the most ancient and most valuable elvish scripture; was it possible? What was her soul merged with? Well that was simple, the dragon. A power to match that of the Lord? What the bloody hell was that meant to mean; if she had the same power as the great creator, then surely she could just destroy the entire planet. Unless she is unaware of this power. And when was she marked by a dark power? Well she has that scar, but nobody knows where it came from, it just appeared next time she was seen alive; unless the elves knew about it?

Hell maybe her choice? That just makes no sense at all. Some of these things are so bloody unhelpful. A scar will wrench her heart, once again, terribly unhelpful. Well one thing is clear; there will be a sacrifice, but a sacrifice of what? And the whole magic thing, well according to the prophecy she will use magic for pretty much everything. So all in all the prophecy is no help at all. Karbith lay for hours thinking everything over. This is how all his nights go, mainly sleepless as he dwelled on Rose. And it seemed to him the more he thought about it, the less it made sense. There were occasions of course where he would make a break through; and then of course he would think it over again and realize it made no sense at all.

So it would seem for King Karbith that he was making little progress in his mission to decipher the prophecy and learn how Rose was to play her part in history; the prophecy was of incredibly little help and he may as well give up trying to figure it out.

Unless; what if when Rose was killed, she went to hell, which of course she would being as she was so evil; what if she was given the choice to remain in hell, or be reincarnated? What if all she had to do was give something in return; perhaps the dragon, or her power, or even herself? What if Rose was no longer a free spirit, What if she was now working for the devil himself? What if the devil was doing the same to thousands of people all over the kingdom, making bargains with them, selling their souls to Satan? What if the devil planned to rage war upon the kingdom, to take over and rise from hell? Then Karbith would not stand a chance, no one could defeat hell. What if the devil granted Rose a power, a power to rule over all so that she could do his bidding? And it would be her choice, her choice would be hell. A scar; the scar on her face may have been given to her by the devil, a mark to show that she belonged to him. If hell rose from the depths then she would loose the dragon, for how could he live in a place like hell, we would all die.

But then Karbith thought about this; how could hell rise, Rose never really died she just went in to hiding, there is no such thing as the devil and if she sacrificed the dragon then she would loose part of herself; so that wouldn't work. And the mark, she probably got that in the fight with the elves, hell could not rise, the devil does not make bargains and he would definitely not grant Rose more power than she already has. So once again Karbith concluded that he had a very vivid imagination and he needed some sleep so that he didn't keep coming up with stupid, bizarre and completely and utterly unrealistic answers; because hell doesn't even exist.

Chapter 20

Laylan's Return

*"If you run from your problems, and look back, you are more likely
to fall. If you face your problems head on then you always know
where you're heading."*

L AYLAN SOARED THROUGH the sky, his great eagle wings flapping
effortlessly. His stunning white head glowed in the bright sunlight;
he was crossing a dense wood, a forest that hid well the city of Elvendin.
It wasn't long before Laylan dropped from the sky and landed in the
centre of a large clearing hidden under the tree's canopy. As his feet
touched the ground, he morphed swiftly back in to his elf form.
He stood there only a second before he found himself faced with
fifty archers, all arrows directed at him. He remained completely still
waiting for Carman to appear. Just as he had assumed, the elf woman
strode in to the open. She stood there so fine before Laylan; he had
an admiration for her, she had led the elves for so long now, almost a
ten years.

"Bit hefty on the old protection front aren't we?" said Laylan
casually.

"Better to be protected." Came Carman's silky reply.

"Protected from what?" Carman did not answer; she merely tilted
her head slightly as though considering him for the first time.

"So you did heed Rose's warning."

"I only took it as a precaution." There was a pause between them; the elven archers remained completely still, waiting for their command to shoot.

"And what is it that you want this time Laylan?"

"I have come to do what I was too scared to do. I have come to claim my title as king of Elvendin." Carman's first reaction was to open her mouth in a stupid, gormless fashion.

"What?"

"I have come to claim the elven throne."

"What right do you have? You abandoned the elves; you turned away from us. Why now do you choose to come back?"

"I have every right; my father and his father, and his fathers father, were all great kings. At the time of my fathers death I was too distraught to except the throne and rule Elvendin. I was eleven; that is no age to take on such a responsibility. Then over time I grew to think of you as a worthy ruler. I deemed it fit to allow you to continue your rule; however, now from what I have seen, I have noted that action must be taken. Members of our race are being captured and tortured, yet you think this expectable? You think that it's ok to sit here in hiding when our brothers and our sisters, and their children are suffering the most brutal torture and the most horrific deaths? How can you live with yourself? We once swore to look after each other, yet now all you do is bury your head in the sand. I am disappointed in you, all of you." He was now addressing the entire assembly of elves. "People we care about, so what if they are not from Elvendin itself, so what if they are not related to us by blood! They are related to us by belief; belief and race! It is now, when times are hard that the Lord told us we would need to unite, for together we are stronger, together we are mighty; but alone, alone we are nothing." Carman now had tears in her eyes; she looked hard at Laylan, and then bowed, she bowed as low as physically able then with one swift movement knelt before him. Laylan saw out of the corners of his eyes that all the surrounding elves had done the same.

"I apologise; I have been blind. I will now follow you my liege." Carman's head was now incredibly close to the ground.

A voice rose from deep within the tree's, "What about the dragon and its rider?"

"They have gone elsewhere; we cannot count on them for help. However do not let this dampen your spirits; we are a magical race, whereas the humans and the dwarves are not."

"But what about Karbith, he uses magic as well?"

"He is one man, we are thousands. Will you all follow me?" From within the trees and the depths of the forest came cries of "Yes!" There was a cry on the wind that echoed the shouts from the elves.

"We must prepare, our finest craftsmen must build grand weapons, bows, arrows, spears, swords and daggers. Our best spell casters must place protective spells around those unable to do so for themselves; and our archers and swordsmen, you must train heavily. Two weeks; two weeks and we will be leaving to fight the humans; should the dwarves also be there, then we will meet them head on. We fight for our families, we fight for our friends, we fight for peace, and we fight for our freedom. Would you rather die fighting for what is right, or die never having tasted freedom, living a dull pointless life? I know which I would choose. The meaning of our existence was to help those who were struggling on their journey's, how can we do that when we cannot even leave the forest; we are betraying the Lord. He has turned his back on us in the past, but perhaps it was only because we turned our backs on him; now we should trust the lord, give our lives to him, after all is he not a lord of creation? Never in any of our scriptures was he named the destructor? Have faith in our God, have faith in each other, and most of all have faith in yourselves. Remember it is not how you walk the path; it's how you fight what faces you. Now go, prepare yourselves, you have two weeks, then we shall gather here; I will check regularly of your progress, and remember life is worth fighting for!"

A great cheer erupted from the elves and they hurriedly left the clearing to begin their preparations for war.

CHAPTER 21

Thalayli's Vision

"Sometimes it only takes a little faith for things to come right."

THALAYLI WAS IN the heart of a great valley far beyond the forest that was home to the elves. The sky was a bright blue and the sun shone down upon the earth making the temperature warm and summery. The dragon lay on the hillside gazing down at a small stream; surrounding the stream were thousands of buttercups, they then spread across the valley making Thalayli's surroundings incredibly yet beautifully yellow.

The dragon had flown all night so was now feeling rather sleepy; however he was finding it hard to sleep since his parting from Rose. He missed her greatly and not a second went by when he did not think about her. Everything he saw, everything he felt, everything he heard, he wanted to share with her. He lived for her; but she had left him. He knew that it had to be done; it was not her fault, she did not do it to hurt him. Thalayli had forgiven Rose for choosing to follow a different path to him; he could not go to Agractabeo, it was not a place for dragons, he knew that. Dragons are pure of heart and soul, not an evil thought will enter their mind, yet Rose, she was completely different; she was made to be both good and evil. She was made to have a choice.

Thalayli closed his eyes, the sun shone so brightly that the light was still visible through his thick eyelids. Behind his lids he could see grey; ignoring the light he drifted into a deep sleep. However it was not long before he was awoken by a voice in his head. *Rise dragon, you must listen to your heart.* Thalayli stirred; he opened his eyes though he did not see the yellow valley where he had fallen asleep. Instead *he saw a* red river of blood; millions of corpses filled the valley, buttercups were no more. Elves, dwarves, humans and other creatures lay dead upon the reddened grass. Abandoned limbs were broken, lonesome on the ground; their owners often meters away from them. The grotesque scene sickened the dragon. He tried to look away, close his eyes but found that his body was unmovable. *This is what will become of the world if you do not help.* Thalayli looked upon the red valley, examining the bodies; there he saw Laylan, Karbith, Dean, Jack, Carman; and then he spotted her, Rose. Her body was smashed and broken. Thalayli roared inside, screamed with pain; all of a sudden the vision seemed real. His heart broke; his soul was torn in two. *You can save her; call upon the dragons, you can stop this.* The voice was deep and confident in the dragon's conscience. Thalayli took one last look at the dead valley then took mastery of his body again. The buttercup valley reappeared; he then leapt into the air and soared through the sky. It was simple in his mind what he had to do; he must find the dragons that went in to hiding years ago.

. . . .

Thalayli flew for days; he crossed valleys, forests, and oceans. Eventually, three days later he landed on the edge of a gigantic mountain. Its peak was covered in thick snow; a blizzard was strong across the mountain making visibility hard especially for Thalayli due to his lack of an eye. He chose to remain on the edge of the mountain for the remainder of the day and did not rise till late into the following day. The blizzard still raged but the dragons strong red and black hide protected him from the snow, and the fire inside his belly kept him warm.

Come the middle of the day the strong, powerful dragon raised his snakelike head in an attempted to penetrate the thick fall off snow and gain a sense of direction. However his eyesight failed him and he deduced to use his other senses to find his way over the mountain in search of the dragons. He searched for days; the blizzard not stopping its attack on the mountain. Thalayli grew tired, his quest to find the dragons now seemed so much more difficult than it had been when he had sat in the yellow valley. Now however the snow beat his face, his vision completely useless. The fire in his belly was the only thing that kept the dragon from giving in to the power of the snow fall. But with the wind going against him, Thalayli was rapidly growing weaker, the huge gust of air would battle against the dragon's wings, often unfurling them and sending him toppling backwards. It took all of Thalayli's last reserves of strength to keep his large bat like wings folded flat against his back. The snow was getting deeper and deeper, the large dragon was now not only fighting the wind, he was fighting the snow draughts. The snow reached the dragons stomach and was pulling at his strength. Thalayli was losing, his strength failed. With one last gust from the wind, the dragon was thrown backwards in to the snow. There he remained, laid in the cold; the fire deep within him was slowly going out. What did he have left? Why should he fight? The blizzard continued and although the dragon was large, it was still not long before his body was covered in a thick layer of snow. The dragon then allowed himself to be consumed by the darkness.

Thalayli was sat on the edge of a hill. From the hillside he could see the entire kingdom. People in this kingdom were free, they were all equal, they respected each other and the only battle they fought was the battle of life. They all appeared so happy. Then he saw her, stood far to his right was Rose. She was completely alone; she was not happy, in fact she had no good emotions left. She felt, to him, angry, scared, bitter, guilty and jealous; all at the same time. Thalayli knew that he was feeling only a fraction of what she was; it was now clear what had happened. Rose was feeling all the bad emotions of the people in the kingdom; she had taken them for herself so that the people below her could be happy. Why? Was this some form of punishment?

Thalayli awoke, he felt fire on is skin and gazed around. He was surrounded by three dragons; they were smaller than him, but he could see that they were quite old.

Who are you dragon? The dragon that had spoken was of a dark blue color, his voice was deep and rough, as though he was growling. The sun was now high in the sky, and the majority of the snow had melted leaving small rivers and streams trickling down the mountainside.

My name is Thalayli; I have come to seek Naranith, Lord of the dragons.
The three dragons gazed at Thalayli quizzically. *Why have you sought our lord?* Said the second dragon that had a glowing hide of gold.

That business is between me and the dragon lord. I must see him it is a matter of urgency. Will you take me to him? Thalayli snaked his long neck round to face the golden dragon.

Yes, I will; however I fear that you may not be able to make the flight, you seem badly injured.

I will make the flight, my body is broken but my spirit is not; I will fly. With that the mighty red and black dragon rose; it took a lot of effort but he did it. The other three dragons looked on as Thalayli fought to take off; once he was hovering a couple of meters off the ground the other dragons leapt effortlessly into the air and prepared to guide him to the dragon lord.

Where are you from then Thalayli? Asked the golden dragon.

The land across the sea, beyond the ancient forest.

You have flown far then, a weeks flight perhaps?

I flew with haste, it took only three days. The dark blue dragon flew closer to Thalayli and the golden dragon to hear their conversation.

Your meeting with the lord must be of great importance to you then Thalayli.

Yes it is.

The conversation ceased as they flew around the mountain revealing a large open valley nestled right in the heart of an incredibly large mountain range. Here was the valley of the dragons; this was where Thalayli's parents had created his egg. This was his home. The valley was green and peaceful; hidden away from the rest of the world. No man could enter this valley for they would be unable to cross the high mountains; they would die trying.

However Thalayli thought little of this as he followed the third of the three dragons to the far side of the valley. This dragon was green; he seemed to melt into the surrounding valley, as though he completely belonged here in the valley of dragons. They flew across a small stream that trickled over grey rocks and wove in and out of small boulders. White lilies grew beside the water gazing at their own reflection. Everything in the valley seemed to radiate an energy of its own, similar to the trees of Elvendin.

Coming into view now was a large cave set in to the foot of a great mountain. It was large enough for several dragons to enter at once. Quite rapidly the green dragon in front began to loose height and Thalayli soon found himself landing. His legs buckled as he hit the ground and he tumbled forward crushing his left wing beneath him. His neck was twisted at a peculiar angle and he could no longer feel his back right leg. Still however he dragged himself upright; his leg hanging limply from his body and his wing flopped down at his side.

Why do you do this dragon? Whispered the green dragon deep from within Thalayli's conscience.

Because I live for one being, and she is now in great danger of loosing herself, I could not bare for that to happen, she means everything to me. I live only for her.

The dragon did not reply; he just inclined his head slightly and turned to enter the cave. Thalayli proceeded into the cave after the green dragon; he found it hard to adjust to the darkness with only one eye, so he paused briefly. The air around him was damp and musty; it had the stench of something long dead.

Still the dragon's eye did not adjust; but then he saw a completely new scene. The cave around him had disappeared and he was stood back on the edge of the bloody valley. However it was different, now the valley was filled with movement. Evil creatures prowled over the dead bodies, drinking their blood and eating their flesh. Demons rose from beneath the ground, soared through the air on a rainbow of different colored wings; their faces monstrous and distorted, their eyes red with anger and hate. They fed upon the destruction of the valley. Then he saw her, among the demons was Rose. She flew at the front of the monster like creatures, alongside another demon; he wore a coat of black leather that streamed behind him as he flew effortlessly through the dark black sky. His hair was a striking white blonde, his eyes a piercing black.

Then as quick as it had happened, Thalayli was back in the cave; he was now surrounded by dragons, at least seven or eight. It was then that he realized that he was on the floor in a heap; he figured he must have collapsed when he had the vision.

He dragged himself upright and looked around; the cave was now filled with silver light, it seemed to radiate from the walls themselves. The dragons that surrounded him were a rainbow of colors; they seemed to glow with a light of their own. They gazed down at him with a deep concern and they all probed at him with their consciences trying to figure if he was ok.

As Thalayli righted himself he noticed a dragon that seemed to radiate more energy than the rest; he was a bright, glowing white. His scales reflected the little light that existed in the cave making him appear to be the source of the light.

Naranith lord of the dragons? asked Thalayli tentatively.

That is I, what is it you seek, chosen one? The white dragon had a voice rich with superiority. It was as though he spoke with a song in his heart.

I need the help of you and your Fastis to aid me and my soul mate in a grave war that is going to infect the entire planet.

And how is it that you have knowledge of this dragon?

I have seen it, in a vision; the lord has given me this gift, I think that I must use it for the greater good. The world is coming to an end Naranith; will you be there when it happens?

I will not be there when it ends; I will be there when the end of the world is prevented. You are the chosen one, we are here to aid you, not now in the time of your great need will I allow myself, or the other dragons, to abandon you.

Thalayli nodded, then his large apparently muscular legs gave way and he lay in a crumpled heap on the floor. The other dragons worked the night through working their magic trying to aid the red and black dragon to a speedy recovery. His wounds were healed, and his muscles repaired, it was only his soul that remained damaged; even in his sleep Thalayli could feel his soul slowly being torn in two. It felt to him as though some one had stroked at his soul with a blade, and it was slowly being cleaved down the centre. It was then in his coma that he deduced that physical wounds were inconsequential, they could be healed over time; however wounds of the soul never healed, they continue over time to grow and eat away at our very existence until there is nothing left of us except an empty shell of existence. It felt to Thalayli as though nothing was left, there was nothing to fight for; he knew that in the end he did not belong to this world, so whether the battle was won or lost, he would still go to the same place. When his work was finished on this planet he would surely move on to another world, as a dragon he was created to serve those who had lost themselves, he had no other purpose than to serve others. The dragon knew that he was not destined to spend eternity with Rose, whether the war went well or ill, he would still have to leave her, or she leave him.

Chapter 22

Ready For War

"Who are we to take claim over land and animal when they belong to no one other than the Lord?"

ROSE WAS STOOD in a large field surrounded by other humans and a few elves and dwarves. Some were perfecting their swordsmanship, some their archery, and some were practicing their magic. From all across the field large flashes of light and bright orbs of energy could be seen filling the plain with a variety of color. The sky was of a dark grey and the air surrounding them held a dampness that seemed to close around them giving them no room to breath. To the north of the field was a large mountain range, the high peaks were obscured by the grey clouds. To the east and west of the field were large forests, they were dark and foreboding as though the very tree's themselves were evil. And to the south lay a thin strip of trees and then the golden sand of the beach.

The people in the meadow were flanked by the Aquilcornilus, their great winged figures shadowing the men and women of the field. They appeared to be aiding the people in their training, offering them advice and giving them encouragement.

Rose drew the cross bow level with her head and took aim towards the target a few hundred feet away. She put all her concentration in to the centre of the wooden target. Rose used magic to set the arrow alight with a black flame; she then drew back the sinew string and prepared to fire the blazing arrow.

"Rose!" Rose felt a hand grab her shoulder; she spun round to face them but in the mean while sent the black arrow shooting skyward. It then landed amongst a group of swordsman; the arrow hit the ground and exploded in a mass of black fire. The screams of burning men echoed across the field; however they were ignored as Rose gazed in to the face of a tall, slender yet well built man. His hair was of a white blonde, his face was, although young, it was wise and seemed full of pain and sorrow. His garb consisted of a red shirt and long black leather jacket, which seemed highly inappropriate for the warmth of the day. He also seemed oddly dressed for the time period in which they were living; he was also wearing black denim jeans and heavy black boots.

"Pyro," Rose snapped, "What the hell are you doing creeping up on me like that?"

"I only wished to see you, get a general idea of your strength; after all we will be fighting side by side."

"Through no choice of my own, I would rather fight alone."

"And you think that you could take on an army of dwarves, elves, humans and dragons, all by your little lonesome?"

"Dragons?"

"Opp's did you not know; your little dragon friend went and paid a visit to the dragon lord, so now Naranith and his Fastis are joining the Great War. Sorry you heard it from me rather than your Master." Rose growled and gave Pyro a glare that penetrated his very soul.

"You should watch your tongue Pyrilious."

"Now it has been a long time since some one used my real name, in fact years; the last person who used it in fact was you." Rose did not reply she just continued to glare at the man before her.

"It has been along time; perhaps too long in fact."

"A life time would not be long enough to not be cursed with your company." Rose retorted, as she snarled at the man before her.

"Ouch I'm really hurt, you actually hurt my feelings."

"Bullshit, you don't have any feelings."

"Oh and I suppose you do?" Once again Rose failed to answer, and continued to glare at Pyro.

"Ah, demons are all the same, no heart, no soul, and no emotions." Pyro made a quick flicking motion with his head, as he did so his face transfigured; now his brow and forehead were severely disfigured. Large deep ridges had appeared and his eyes were a dark black, no color existed in them. His teeth grew sharp and predator like, he seemed to grow in stature and he became more muscular and he no longer seemed as slender as before. From his back sprouted large black feathered wings that he stretched out and shook slightly as though they had been cramped up for a long time.

Rose looked at him cautiously and a quiet growl erupted from her. "It's hard isn't it Rose, you've been fighting it for so long now; you've been hiding who you really are." Rose remained silent, as though she was fighting a secret battle, her body was shaking slightly and her demeanor was tense.

"You can't fight it any more, you are who you are; you can't keep running." Rose's breath became sharp and shallow, and then she just relaxed and allowed her body to go through the same changes as Pyro.

"You see, it's what you are, an animal." With a deep roar Rose lunged towards Pyro. He caught her and held her close to him as their lips met; they remained like this for a while before together disappearing in to the woods.

．．．．．．．．．．．．．．．．．．．．．．．．．．．．

The sky was now of a deep purple and twilight was nigh. The mass of beings from within the field had now congregated nearer to the mountains. They appeared to be gathered around a large boulder in which was stood a tall, muscular man with dark brown hair and livid green eyes; a soft breeze causing his flowing black cloak to ripple behind him. To his left hand side stood what appeared to be the strongest of the Aquilcornilus, his skin was dark, almost black, making his eyes appear whiter than that which is classed as usual. He had an incredibly unnatural amount of muscle and he stood at around seven feet tall. His wings were folded neatly behind him and could be seen rising upwards making him appear even taller.

The man stood upon the boulder leant towards the large beast of a man beside him, "Where are they, they should be here by now?"

"I do not know Master; they were seen walking in to the forest at about mid-day." The Aquilcornilus' voice was deep and rough, almost a growl. At this news the man upon the boulder roared. "Rose! Pyro!"

Deep within the forest, on the other side of the field, lay Rose and Pyro. At the sound of the roar the pair of them leapt to their feet. "Oh bloody hell!" said Pyro miserably. He had retaken his human form and he turned to look through the trees to where the mass had congregated.

Rose scrambled around for her clothes and hurried to pull them on. Pyro now did the same and swore heavily under his breath. "Man you're in trouble now," he said once he had run out of significant foul words.

"I'm in trouble! I'm in trouble? If anyone's in trouble its you."

"Why me, your his closest?"

"More of a reason for me to get away with it whilst you get punished."

"I don't think it's going to be that simple, you mean more to him than anyone, he feels for you." Pyro had said this in a barely audible whisper. Rose stepped away from him and walked out of the forest. "Well bollocks to you then bitch, just walk off and leave me to face the music; we could have at least walked over there together." Pyro sprinted after her pulling on his coat as he did so.

The dark skinned creature beside the boulder looked out across the field where he then spotted Rose and Pyro. He pointed this out to his master, who then replied with a snarl and a growl.

Rose strode up to the man upon the boulder and stood squarely in front of him. She looked him straight in the eye, yet remained silent.

"You serve me Rose, not any one else." Tension rose and the mass of creatures surrounding them looked on in a wary silence.

"You owe me; I reached in to hell and raised you from its murky depths; for that you should be grateful." This came out as a fierce growl that caused the crowd to step back in fear.

"I am grateful Abbadon, and I serve you well; however, not once in our little deal did you once say anything about not being aloud to having sex with whom I like." Mumbling was sounded by the surrounding beings and all eyes now turned to Pyro. "Whoah, don't bring me in to this; I had nothing to do with it," he said lifting his hands submissively.

"Ah, Pyro; I think you are very much involved here. Please stand before me." Abbadon beckoned for Pyro to stand beside Rose. He skulked forwards and stood to her right, and hung his head.

"Looking at the floor instead of looking at those in which you are addressing is a sign of weakness," growled Abs. Pyro's head shot up and he looked Abs directly in the eye.

"Sorry, I just found the ground more appealing to the eye than your face; forgive me if I, to you, appeared weak." Pyro spat and turned in to his demon form. He flexed his wings and let out a vicious roar. If there was one thing that annoyed Pyro the most it was being classed as weak; he had been a demon long enough to know that he was one of the strongest when in his true form.

"Now that Pyro, is why I chose you for my army; your vicious side. If you and Rose sleeping together adds to your more animal side, then continue; for the battle that we are facing will need the animosity that you two have." He nodded at Rose and Pyro to join him on the right hand side of the boulder. They did so and Pyro retook his human form.

"My people, I have saved you all from your miserable fates; I have given you hope when you thought there was none. I have been there for you when all of those around you, the people you loved had abandoned you. I have raised some of you from the bloody depths of hell, and others I have rescued from their miserable lives here on earth. I have given you a power above others; now please those that have journeyed here to escape their lives, step forward. It is now that I shall grant you your final gift, Immortality." Almost a third of the mass stepped forward; the rest all receded to allow room for the others.

Abbadon raised his hand and directed his palm at the awaiting army. "Now your true colors shine; you will have your vengeance on life." A great black energy shot from his palm, showering the creatures. Immediately the beings began to grow, dwarves were now of an equal height to that of the elves and the humans. Great wings of varying colors rose from their now muscular backs. Their foreheads were now wrinkled and disfigured, and their teeth were now large and more pointed. All the beings were now fully formed demons, Abs had created an army of animals; full of hate and anger, with a thirst for revenge. The army erupted in an almighty roar. Together their sound was heard even back on the mainland. The roar shook the very earth they stood on and the air vibrated with the sound waves.

Abbadon smiled, a dark, sinister grin; his green eyes flashed black for a second, showing the darkness within.

CHAPTER 23

Rage Of The Rider

"There is always a reason behind someone's madness; remember in their eyes what they are doing is right. So next time just stop and think; how would you react if you had seen what they had."

NENAMIS AND SARABIE soared through the sky; the forest was drawing nearer. The red dragon began to circle above the trees trying to find the easiest way to gain entry through the forest canopy. Sarabie's eye gushed with blood and it was now that she realized she could not see out of it. Nenamis picked up on this and showed his concern to her conscience. The dragon dove into the forest and landed neatly in the same clearing that Sarabie and Laylan trained in.

The elf was sat to the side of the clearing; his legs were folded and his hands rested on his knees with his palms facing upwards. He opened his eyes and took in the pair. He noted Sarabie's wound and leapt up to her aid.

"Are you ok, what happened; is he dead?" He ran towards up to her, stopped and then went to place a finger on her wound. Stung by his touch, Sarabie batted his hand away.

"Yes he's dead, and I'm fine leave me alone."

"Sarabie wait! I want to help you, please tell me what happened." Sarabie didn't answer she only glared at him; the thumping in her head beginning to drive her insane.

Laylan was slightly hurt and he gazed at her with concern. "Please tell me what happened."

"Did you know?"

"Know what?" answered Laylan trying to sound innocent even though he knew what was coming.

"What it would do. Did you know that by killing him, I killed part of myself?" Sarabie looked at him, longing for him to say that he had not known. After all that she had been through she thought that at last she had found some one she could trust. However as she gazed in to his eyes she saw how wrong she had been.

"I knew. I am sorry."

"Do you know how it feels? The pain; it doesn't stop, it never ceases. Its constant; and the drumming, oh the pain in my head. Why? Why won't it stop?" Sarabie burst in to tears as she clawed at her head, as though trying to pull the flesh from her very skull.

"I am truly sorry." Laylan hung his head; he could not bare to face her now knowing what he must do. He was sorry, and he truly hated himself for what he had allowed to happen.

"You're not sorry!" Sarabie screamed. Her once brown eyes now turning in to a deep black as the soul behind them disappeared.

"I hate you! I hate the elves! I hate this forest! And I hate life for what it has done to me! I hate God and the supposed angels! I hate you all! And I will destroy you all!" Laylan looked at Sarabie, a tear running down his face. All he wanted was to hold her and make her feel safe; but he knew that she would not understand that any more. The being before him was no longer human. It was a hurricane of destruction that had to be stopped.

Then as quickly as she had begun Sarabie stopped. She slumped to the ground sobbing uncontrollably. Laylan gazed at her for a moment then knelt beside her and put his arm across her shoulder.

"I want to be alone; Laylan please leave me be." With that Sarabie rose and strode out of the glen. Nenamis followed after her giving Laylan a glare, similar to that of Sarabie's, as though her pain and injury was his fault. The elf was unaware of how to proceed so decided to confide in Carman as quickly as possible.

Sarabie was not far from the clearing before she collapsed. Nenamis nudged her gently with the tip of his giant nose.

It has troubled you greatly; there is more damage than just your eye.

My soul, it feels as though a part of it has been torn off, like I'm no longer whole. But how can that be? The great dragon shook his head and gently lifted Sarabie up by his teeth and carried her back to the tree house.

Once there he settled her in her bed. He waited until she was deep in sleep before leaving the tree in search of answers.

. . . .

Laylan sat on the boulder like bench waiting for Carman. It took her a while to appear and when she did so a broad grin was worn upon her face.

"The deed is done; and I believe that the majority of the congratulations should be awarded to you; after all you put all the work in to gain her trust." Carman sat beside Laylan and gazed at the small snowdrop filled clearing.

"What has it done to her?" the elf snapped suddenly.

"I'm sorry I don't quite understand."

"You know bloody well what I mean; killing him, it's done something to her. It's broken her."

"Well yes of course it's changed her, but for the better I think."

"What has it done to her?" as he said this Laylan stood and drew a fine, elegant blade from his hip and with one swift movement had it placed across Carman's neck.

"Her soul; every time you kill someone a part of your soul dies too."

"And you still let her do it? Is this why we never made a move on Garston?"

"Yes, we elves are too pure to go round tearing of pieces of our souls, but Sarabie; she is, part human. However I did not realise it would effect her as it does us elves. However you could say she is disposable, and after all the major threat now is gone. We have no more evil to fight; therefore Sarabie's duty is done."

"Her duty? How can you say that, she has given us her life, in fact no, more than that; her soul." Laylan pressed the blade harder

163

onto Carman's neck so that a small droplet of blood trickled down her skin.

"Her duty, as said in the prophecy was to right wrongs; it's over now."

"So you're just going to brush her aside and abandon her?"

"No, but she cannot stay here in Elvendin; after all she has tasted blood, her soul is no longer whole. What's to stop her killing again, what's to stop her killing one of us?"

"And you knew all along what would happen to her, you sent a sixteen year old to kill her own father just because you didn't want to damage yourself or one of your precious people. What gives you the right to dictate someone's life, you have ruined her entire existence merely because of your cowardice and the fact that you seem to think that elves are superior to other races."

"But we are superior; can't you see, we know the true path of life. We were placed on the earth by the creator so that we could show others the way because they are blind."

"No, you're the blind one Carman. Through your ignorance you are ruining other people's lives instead of making them better. You say we are here to help, yet where ever you go, you only seem to bring destruction. And you think that you are guiding others on their paths, you barely leave the bloody forest. You are completely oblivious to those around you, and are so stuck up your own arse you can't even see where your going or what you are doing." At this Carman grabbed Laylan's wrist and twisted the blade away from her throat.

"How dare you; after your father died I took care of you when no one else would. Remember you chose your position; so don't you dare comment on how I chose to rule the elves. If that is your opinion then I think it is in all our best interests if you left."

"You know what, for the first time I think you are actually speaking sense. I will leave, after I have told Sarabie exactly what you have done to her."

There is no need, I shall do that myself. Carman and Laylan both looked up to see Nenamis turning back into the depths of the forest.

"Great," said Carman. "Now look what you have done." She snapped at Laylan as she spun to face him, a ferocious look upon her face. Laylan merely smiled, "It is about time someone told her the truth."

Carman growled and stalked away, "I don't want to see you in Elvendin again Laylan."

Laylan watched her leave, waited to make sure she did not return, then followed Nenamis back towards Sarabie.

. . . .

Sarabie woke to find Nenamis gazing at her from the other side of the tree house. He had used his mind to wake her and she felt the urgency in his conscience.

What is it Niver Nenamis? What troubles you?

It is Carman; you have been deceived, in fact we have both been deceived.

What do you mean?

She knows what has happened to you, your soul; it has broken; when you kill your soul breaks. Each time someone dies due to your hand, a part of your soul is broken, and it is discarded. Due to the death of Garston, your soul has now been broken; it will not be the same again. As Nenamis thought this Sarabie remained still in shock; she could not quite believe what the great dragon was saying.

So she knew all along that I would be hurt?

Yes, that is why she would not allow herself or any of her people to kill Garston; to her it was easier for a complete stranger to kill him that it was someone she knew.

So she allowed me to suffer. I knew something was different, like I was bad somehow, gone wrong. The drumming; the pain. I can still feel it inside you Sarabie?

And now you know. Sarabie growled in answer. *I will not let her get away with this; she will suffer just as I will now suffer for the rest of my life.*

Nenamis did not reply, in fact he did not even agree; however he knew by the strength of her thoughts that her decision was final. It was his love for her that allowed him to remain still as she mounted him and prepared for war against the elves.

Thump, Thump, Thump.

Thump, Thump, Thump.

Thump, Thump, Thump.

The drumming never stops.

The pain never stops.

. . . .

Laylan ran through the woods, ducking under branches and leaping over shrubs. His heart raced as he feared for the worst; how would she react? He was the only one who truly knew the extent of her power. He saw the tree house appear from behind a large fresh green pine tree. It was as he feared Sarabie was already sat astride Nenamis, sword in hand; he could feel her anger from the distance in which he still had to cover. Sarabie's feeling of betrayal could be felt in the air; it seemed to tremble as though it knew what was to transpire. Laylan also shook with a feeling of dread; the false trust in which he had built with the dragon rider was now shattered; she would no longer heed his advice, or perhaps even acknowledge him at all.

However his thought of being ignored was proved false; Sarabie saw him approaching. She drew and pointed her fathers sword at him and growled, "How dare you return to me?"

"I am truly sorry, I . . . ."

"I don't want your apology, I want your blood."

"Sarabie, no; do not turn in to the killer that Carman things you will become. Its not who you are."

"Well tell me, who am I? What is the point of me being here? After all I have completed my purpose; I have nothing left; so how about I punish you all for the pain that you have caused me. It feels to me that my father's murder was not enough to fore fill my thirst for revenge; in fact it has only increased it." Sarabie glowered at the elf before her. "What am I, I am not my own person; my life is dictated by those around me. Well not any more."

"Please don't do this, it will destroy you."

"Then let it be, for I would rather destroy myself now and not have to spend a second longer in this world, than allow myself to be ruled for the rest of my completely pointless existence and never fore fill my thirst for revenge. I don't want to be here a moment longer."

"Then so be it; kill me first, then you can move on to the rest of my race. Then if it pleases you, you can continue on to the humans and the dwarves. Or perhaps you might not even stop there; you may even go on to destroy the entire planet. But answer me this, once you have started, will you stop?"

Sarabie glared at Laylan, she seemed no longer herself; she now seemed to resemble some one possessed. The truth of it was that she was possessed, she was possessed by hate, anger and the hunger for inflicting pain upon others.

"If I destroyed the world then at least no one would suffer any more like I suffered." For the moment it took her to say this, Laylan saw a hint of the old Sarabie, her eyes seemed to soften and her gaze drifted briefly. Laylan now had a small fragment of hope that perhaps Sarabie was not completely over ruled by her emotions; however her old self showed only briefly and had rapidly vanished from her face.

"Then start with me, kill me; for you see I believe that you are our only hope. Garston was only the beginning of a long line of evil. This world needs you, please do not abandon it. But should you chose to adhere to your current decision then I would rather die now, than live in a world with out the real you. So please go ahead, get it over with." Laylan spread his arms out wide and closed his eyes and waited for her to strike her blow. However it did not come.

"I will not kill you Laylan." With that Nenamis took to the skies leaving the elf alone in the forest, tears streaming down his faces, his body shaking violently.

. . . .

"I can hear the children, the children the children,
I can hear the children. The children cry.
I can hear the children, the children, the children,
I can hear the children, the children die."

Sarabie was stalking through the forest; blade in hand. Nenamis hovered over head keeping look out for Carman. Sarabie, in the next clearing, could hear a group of children playing. She sheathed her sword and peered around the trees. There, before her where around ten elven children. They pranced around the clearing, singing and dancing with one another.

"I can hear the children, the children the children,
I can hear the children. The children cry.
I can hear the children, the children, the children,
I can hear the children, the children die."

Sarabie stepped out from behind the trees, and with one swift movement of her wrist left the ten children slaughtered upon the ground.

She lifted her chin and let out a deep breath, a half smile half snarl across her face. As she walked to the other side of the clearing she walked amongst the children. When passing one she made a deliberate kick, at one of the child's heads; and the smile broadened as its face crushed beneath her foot.

Nenamis landed beside her and gazed at her sadly. He loved her and was always there for her; however he knew what she was doing was wrong. Yet his heart over came his head and he allowed her to mount him as they went in search for Carman.

. . . .

Carman was preparing the elves for Sarabie; she knew that she alone could not defeat a pissed of rider. She stood in the centre of a large open clearing deep in the heart of the forest. Archers were assembled in the tree tops and swordsmen surrounded the edge of the clearing forming a ring around Carman. The elves that were more advanced with their magic stood beneath the trees with their backs against the tree trunks.

"Sarabie has turned; her soul has been torn as we all knew well it would. However evil has become her, and therefore for the good of the earth we must destroy her. Fight for your lives my people, for she will have no sympathy; evil has no limits, so nor does she.

You all know the plan as discussed previously before Garston's death; we knew this would happen so please keep faith and stick to the plan."

Carman stood by the nearest pine tree along with several other magicians. She gazed in the direction in which she assumed Sarabie would come. However she spent little time gazing as above the clearing, high over the forest canopy she heard a deep and very vicious roar. She looked up at the sky and saw movement above them. Just as she thought she could glimpse Nenamis, a stream of black flame came dancing towards them. The fire flew around the clearing, twisting and fighting its way through the trees. Slowly it began to fade and Carman saw the damage that was left behind. Many of the swordsmen lay dead and scorched upon the ground. The trees were now blackened and burnt and some of the archers situated lower in the trees branches also now lay dead.

Carman was taken aback with shock; she looked about herself taking in the scene. Half her army were already dead and she began to wonder if perhaps Sarabie could be destroyed. The tree canopy was broken as Nenamis soared through it and landed with a large thud upon the ground causing a small earth quake.

"You all betrayed me, you all knew what would happen, and not one of you tried to save me; to rescue me from this fate. All you cared about was saving yourselves; you didn't care if one person got hurt in the process." Sarabie yelled at the surrounding elves, tears streaming down her face.

"You all abandoned me when I needed you most; not one of you cared. If the world is full of people like you then is it really worth saving. You don't deserve life, not one of you." Sarabie leapt from Nenamis and strode towards Carman.

"We will not let you destroy anything or anyone. I am sorry Sarabie but it is you who must be destroyed." Carman said this in a whisper as Sarabie drew closer.

"You seemed to think that one kill would destroy me."

"Well hasn't it?"

"No my soul is stronger than any of yours; I was fine until I found out the truth. It was you that tore my soul apart; and now because of you and your ignorance you will die. You have no idea what its like. Its as though some one has delved their fist in to your chest and is crushing your heart so it feels that your heart is no longer beating. The drumming in my head. It never stops, its always there." Once again Sarabie began to tear at her head.

"Then how about I end your pain, attack!" with that all the archers left in the trees fired flaming arrows towards Nenamis. Sarabie spun round and fended off the attack with a flick of her wrist. However with her attention caught on the arrows she did not notice the hundreds of spells shooting their way towards the dragon. Blue and white light twisted through the air; the light lifted Nenamis from the ground, his body spun in the air and with a huge crack is neck broke and he thudded back to the ground. The ground shook with the force and even the trees seemed to groan with the pressure upon the earth. The dragon's wings were bent and broken, and his neck was twisted and folded at a harsh and unnatural angle. His eyes were glassy and lifeless.

Sarabie ran over to him screaming. She collapsed in a heap and began to caress his large, fantastic head. Tears streamed down her face as she looked in to his eyes.

"Please don't leave me," she whispered. "I can't do this with out you; you're my everything." Sarabie felt Nenamis's conscience ebbing away; then it was gone torn away from her and she was alone. Her mind felt empty, and felt that she had no one; she was alone in a world that was against her. Her heart was broken and she felt as though her whole existence was meaningless. The drumming continued, but there were no soothing words of comfort from the dragon. No emotions, no knowledge, no strength. He was gone, and the small fragments of Sarabie's soul began to scream as her heart slowly died with the dragon. All of a sudden even revenge did not seem worth the effort. To Sarabie life now felt completely dead. The pain consumed her as she held his head in her arms.

"I can't do this alone." She gave a huge sob, her body shaking and her face wet from tears.

"Do it," screamed Sarabie. "Kill me, get it over with. I don't want to live any more." And with that Carman pulled a bow from across her back, fitted it with an arrow and aimed it at her heart.

"Very well," Carman released the arrow and it pierced Sarabie's heart. Sarabie felt the arrow shoot through her flesh; she lay down across Nenamis's head and slowly felt life escape her.

She looked in to the dragon's dead eyes and with her last breath whispered, "I love you."

CHAPTER 24

The Call Of War

**"If death was the end then what would be the
point in life?"**

K ARBITH WAS WALKING down the marble staircase of his rather
elaborate castle, when a young boy of no older than ten came
running towards him. The boy was dressed in rich red clothes that
were trimmed with gold. He stopped before the king and bowed low
almost doubling up on himself.

"Sire, I have a message for you; it comes from the guards outside
the castle. They say an elf has come seeking your audience."

Karbith thought briefly before answering, "very well, lead him to
the castle, I shall meet him in the courtyard." The boy bowed low
before turning and hurrying out of the castle doors.

Karbith had come along way in the past few weeks; his army was
now fully developed and the town surrounding the castle rung with the
sound of sparring swords, and the hammer and tongs of blacksmiths
forging armor. Dean had organized the army into platoons and they
were currently out in the fields practicing maneuvers.

Karbith had also learnt to decipher the elvish book of his. However
he was not to happy with the out come. Although on the other hand
he now knew that Rose was not the one spoken of in the prophecy;

he knew this because the book was in the form of a diary. Therefore it told of events that had foregone, this then told him that the dragon and rider spoken of in the book were in fact dead, murdered by the elves. This of course was fantastic news for Karbith. Yet still the great king had a slight nagging feeling that he was missing something. He had read the majority of the book and felt that he needn't read any more as he knew what he needed to know about the prophecy. All he needed to know was that the prophecy did not contain him, which of course it did not. However unbeknown to him, it was written in the book about another second rider; this perhaps would have been of greater importance to him than the prophecy, yet due to the headache and frustration building in him as he attempted to translate elvish, he chose to give up on the book and try his luck on the future.

Karbith now sat on the edge of the water fountain in the centre of the courtyard waiting for the elf. It was not long before the elf appeared. He was tall and lanky, very finely built. He walked with a slender grace as though he floated along rather than walk. He bowed slightly to Karbith before saying, "I have been chosen by my Lord to declare war on you and your army. We have seen the trouble you have caused and the murder and pain you have inflicted upon our people and your own; therefore for the good of the earth we feel we must act. It is apparent that there is no negotiation due to the fact that you will us off the Earths face, therefore only war will suffice."

Karbith nodded slightly, "I agree, the eastern valley. You have three weeks."

"No, one week." And with that the elf turned and drifted off out of the courtyard.

"Bloody cheek, didn't even tell me his name."

Karbith ambled out of the courtyard and through the town. He decided to personally check on the progress of the weaponry. He found it all to his standard so preceded to the training fields at the front of the town. Here he met with Dean.

"Good afternoon Sire," said Dean bowing slightly. "I hope you find our progress satisfactory."

Karbith nodded then answered, "Yes, I do; however there is a slight change in plan. We will not need to seek the elves after all, they have come to us. We will meet them in the face of war in a week from today on the eastern shore. I believe you know of the valley that resides there?"

"I do sir."

"Then we will let their blood form a river in the heart of the valley, may the grass turn red as we extinguish there meaningless existences."

"Yes Sire that is what we would hope."

"Very well, mote it be." Karbith nodded then strode back towards the castle. The preparations were made and war would be his rise.

. . . .

The dwarf Lord sat perched precariously on his oversized throne. His incredibly short legs dangled hopelessly as he addressed his court. A number of around twenty dwarves stood before him as his painfully high pitched whistle of a voice echoed around the hall.

"Although I dislike Rose muchly I am at liberty to trust that in which she says. Only the truth has ever left her lips, so therefore I fear to say that we must ride to war. Lookouts have spotted both human and elven armies crossing the plains. It is therefore my estimate that they will be at war within the next few days. However, fear not as dwarves we are always readily prepared for war. Our time has come men to show to the world that we are half full, not as some would say half empty. We will fight for our freedom at last, that which our ancestors have been planning for centuries. We will have our freedom. Our weapons are strife and our armies ready. Now kind sir's ready your platoons. We will attack when their battle is heavy; when both elves and humans have suffered many casualties, that is when they will be weakest. Therefore we ride in seven days."

The short but stocky audience of dwarves grunted in deep muffled voices and turned to exit the hall.

. . . .

Far away on the island of Agractabeo the army of demons was at its peak strength. The entire army had gathered as before around the large black boulder. Abbadon stood upon it and gazed out at his army with a sinister grin which showed his pride and sense of power.

"My people; my good, strong faithful people. Our time has come at last. Let hell rise and overcome the horrors of the earth. Here you are all amongst friends, here you are appreciated for the beings that you are. Take your revenge on those that have caused you the most pain. Rid the world of their evil. Let the world become ours. The Lord of the earth will shower the world in his tears as we overcome his creation, it will become ours.

Now I have chosen three of you to lead; these three I have chosen for their skill and their thirst for revenge. Now this is because my fellow demons, it is our emotions that give us the most power. It is our fear, anger and hate that drives us. These three I feel have the strongest emotions of all my army. I have chosen, Rose, Pyro and Jack. Now please step forward and claim your titles as captains." From the midst of the crowd strode Rose and Pyro, and from the front walked Jack. All three stood before their Master and bowed low.

"You my friends will lead this army in to the midst of war; you will guide them when they waver from their path of destruction. Just remember my people, the people of the earth have caused you pain, no one deserves to suffer as you have. They inflicted upon you suffering in which you did not deserve, know go; take your power and your strength and destroy those that sought to destroy you." Abs pointed to the far shore of the island, where far in the distance the kingdom could be seen over the vast expanse of ocean. Rose grinned at Pyro and Jack; she then took her demon form. Black wings rose from her back and her forehead became wrinkled and deformed. Fangs erupted from behind her fine lips and she seemed to grow in stature.

Pyro and Jack did the same. Then as one the three of them leapt up in to the skies, followed by the vast army of at least a thousand demons.

. . . .

Naranith was stood over Thalayli as he slowly began to wake. The red and black dragon opened his one eyelid and gazed up at the white dragon. *Thalayli, how long have you had these visions?*

Since I lost my eye.

I see, well we are flying to war. I have heard many disturbing things since you have slept, and one of them is that the war was closer than we first thought.

I believe it to be a matter of days before the battle begins. We do however have a bigger problem; there appear to be four different armies, fighting for four different reasons. This is difficult to comprehend, for I wish not for anyone to suffer; after all us dragons were put here to protect the world. Therefore I find it necessary to fly at once. However my feelings are that you are still not up to your full strength, am I correct?

Yes Naranith, I am afraid you are. However I will fly with you; if there is one thing I have learnt since my time on earth, is that emotion drives us, not strength or power.

The white dragon hummed and nodded. *Spoken from the heart of a warrior. Now will you rise, we must fly at once, the army of Agractabeo has taken flight already; we must hurry if we are not to be too late.* Thalayli stretched out his long neck and staggered to his feet. Together the two dragons left the cave where outside they were greeted by fifty or so awaiting dragons. Many of them showed their condolences towards Thalayli as his empty eye socket remained dark and hollow and he walked with a heavy limp.

My fellow dragons, I feel that this is our last mission, lets get it right. Now to the skies, let's save the world. Naranith roared and leapt in to the sky, followed by the other dragons. Together they appeared as a rainbow in the sky as they streaked through the air faster than any other creature could.

Chapter 25

Maybe He Will Be Better

"If at first you don't succeed, don't worry;
we can't be good at everything."

LAYLAN FOUND THE child exactly where he was supposed to be. The young Karbith was sat outside the cottage with his carers picking at the flowers in the garden. The young boy was no older than thirteen and he appeared bored with life and seemed to enjoy the torture in which he was inflicting upon the daisies before him.

As the elf approached the boy, the boy got up. He watched intently as Laylan approached before shouting, "You're an elf."

"Yes Karbith, I am an elf. I am here to teach you the art of magic in the hope that one day you can stop the ending of my race and yours; do you want to learn magic?"

"Oh yes please. I always knew I was special."

"Ah, now being able to use magic is nothing special, there are quite a few people that can use it. However there are certain things that can be done with magic, that are very special indeed."

One of Karbith's carers rose and shook Laylan's hand. "We have been waiting for you ever since we found his mothers letter and heard of Sarabie's death." She said the last part of this in a whisper; however Karbith had failed to notice.

Laylan was pulled away by Karbith's carer as she said, "You're sure he's ready for this? I don't want the same thing happening to him that happened to his sister."

"Sarabie was different, she was destined to die; it was her path, someone with her power should not live, else the world would come to a very terrible end. Karbith however, he has less power, but when the time comes for the races to unite it is vital that he knows of the history of the elves."

And so it was that Karbith began his training. It was less intensive than Sarabie's had been and he was slower on the uptake. However several years later when he reached the age of seventeen Karbith was fully educated in the use of magic. It was on the day of his seventeenth birthday that he asked the question that had been on his mind for several years.

"Master Laylan, how did my father die?"

"Your father was murdered. He had committed many wrongs in the past and had upset many people. However through his death came the creation of your magical journey."

"Who killed him?"

"The person who killed your father will not be named by me; however I will say that his murder was organized by the elves. I am sorry if this is not what you wanted to hear, however I have made a vow to lie to no one, and deceive no one." Karbith hung his head.

"Were you there when it was ordered?"

"Yes."

"Please leave Laylan. I feel that our training has come to a close, please don't come back." Laylan rose and said, "I am sorry, I truly am." Laylan strode out of the garden and headed back towards the forest.

Karbith remained in the garden for many hours trying to comprehend what Laylan had said. The elves had killed his father, or rather ordered him to be killed. But who had actually killed him?

And so it was that the destruction began.

Chapter 26

Hell And Back Again

"One thing I do not believe in, is imagination. This is because the human mind is not capable of coming up with something from nothing. Therefore perhaps there is an edge of reality to even the wildest of dreams."

SARABIE THOUGHT THAT her death was the end, yet bizarrely enough it wasn't. In fact it was the beginning of something horrid. She opened her eyes; no they were already open; weren't they. She tried to blink though she now found that she had no eyelids to blink with. In fact she found that she had nothing to forgo any moving of any kind with what so ever. So what did that mean, was she dead. However she could think and feel that was definite. She now noted that she wasn't breathing, so did that mean she couldn't talk. This induced some curiosity, so therefore she tried to shout. Nothing. Well this she found terribly unhelpful. So she had no body, just a floating Sarabie soul. No senses, so that meant she couldn't even hear, see, smell or touch. Well that was rather tedious. But even though Sarabie had no body, she could still hear the Thump, Thump, Thump; and she could still feel her soul being torn apart. The pain was unbearable as always but Sarabie could take no actions to attempt to alleviate her stress even though it would have failed to have worked any way. Deep inside Sarabie screamed as the drumming continued. Thump, Thump, Thump. The girl growled with in herself with frustration.

How long had she been her now? A minute? An hour? A day Perhaps? To Sarabie it felt like an eternity. Thoughts kept going over and over in her head; everything she had ever been through. Her father, the death of her Mother, being alone in the cell for so many years, the elves, Laylan, and the death of Niver Nenamis, the only one she had ever truly trusted.

But then something happened that changed things slightly. Far away, as though at the other end of a tunnel she heard a voice. It sound like someone was crying. Well what did Sarabie care of that, it was no concern of hers, she had no body or anything. So why should she worry about someone crying; as far as she was concerned they could suffer on their own, she didn't want to help. Then all of a sudden she was overcome with a feeling of loss. The memory of Nenamis's death struck her like another arrow to the heart. She felt like crying however could not due to the lack of tears and a face for the tears to run down. This then made her feel incredibly angry. Why had she been dumped here? Why was she left in this void? Why were the elves so cruel to here? Why was the world so cruel? All she had ever known all her life was pain and suffering, so did that mean that hundreds of other people out there in the world were suffering? Well if I was alive, she thought, I would kill them all. That would stop the pain and the suffering, and at the same time punish those that were cruel.

It was then that Sarabie felt a sudden strength. But still she could feel her soul being ripped apart, and still she could hear the drums, Thump, Thump, Thump. Why wouldn't it stop? It was then that she heard someone whisper quite close to her.

"How would you like to come with me? I can grant you what you seek; all you have to do is come with me. I can stop the Pain, I can stop the drums." The voice was smooth and silky, as though the person saying it was almost singing. Sarabie tried to talk, yet could not. She wanted to come with this stranger, anywhere was better than here.

Then she heard the person who had screamed shout, "Don't do it. Don't go with him. He is evil, he is the devil. He will take you to hell, don't go with him. Just wait, the doors of heaven will open!"

"I want revenge!" Sarabie all of a sudden found a voice deep within herself. As she said it she felt herself being pulled downwards.

She then realized that she had felt something. So that meant she must have a body. She opened her eyes and found herself in what appeared to be the heart of a volcano. Sarabie was overcome with peace at being released from the pain and the insanity being caused by the drumming. She sat crumpled upon the rocky, ash covered ground. The air was humid and stiflingly hot. However the heat did not bother her at all. It was then that she noted that she was completely naked; now this didn't bother her at all until she stood up and saw stood before her a tall well built man. He appeared to be in his early twenties perhaps a tad younger. His hair was dark and his face slender and angular. He was dressed all in black with a long black cloak, and it was apparent that he dressed not for the current time period. Sarabie glanced at him and he grinned.

"Very nice," he said in a smooth confident voice. He cocked his head slightly then nodded towards her. Sarabie was now dressed in a silk black dress that clung to her figure.

"My name is Abaddon, you however may call be Abs."

"Where am I?" growled Sarabie, her voice tainted with anger and a hint of fear.

"Some may call this hell; however they would be mistaken. This is the centre of the earth. I felt your presence when you were lost in the void between here and heaven. I could only assume that heaven had rejected you. May I ask what is it that you seek?" Abs walked steadily towards Sarabie and ran a finger down the scar upon her face. Sarabie shuddered and stepped back.

"I seek destruction."

"I seek the same, I can feel what you feel Sarabie; I can see your reasoning and I understand. How would you like a second chance?" Sarabie lifted her chin and looked Abs directly in the eye.

"I see, you also want for the dragon to return to you. That I can grant you; however when I call upon you, you must come to me. No argument, no questioning. My will is for the people of the earth to be destroyed; I have lived up there for many years, and I have felt the pain. I wish for the suffering to stop; every day someone is tortured whether it be physical or emotional. I try to save all those that have suffered so that we can unite and together rid the world of evil. Trust me, we both want the same." He looked down on Sarabie, and she could not help but to trust him, he had saved her from the void, was going to bring Nenamis back, and was going to help her achieve her biggest and strongest desire.

"Yes," she said. "I want to go back; I will come to you when the time comes."

"Oh brilliant, how marvelous. Well that's business out of the way; let me introduce you to my right hand man." Abs led Sarabie out of the chamber and down a tunnel which led into a second chamber. The chamber was empty except for an athletically built man who was stood by the far side apparently admiring the wall of rock.

"Pyro! Let me introduce Sarabie, Sarabie this is Pyro. When the time comes you will fight alongside each other." Pyro bowed yet kept his eyes on hers.

"I hope you know what you're letting yourself in for." Pyro's voice was deep yet smooth. However Sarabie took an instant dislike to the man and chose to scowl at him before answering, "I can look after myself and make my own decisions."

"That's good to hear." Pyro tried to smile, however his mutual dislike only produced a scowl to match Sarabie's.

"Right ok then, slight tension; heavy atmosphere. Not to worry, I'm sure you two will be best pals in no time. Now Sarabie I have a gift for you, do please close your eyes." Sarabie did as she was told reluctantly; this was not due to lack of trust in Abs, it was a lack of trust in Pyro.

Abs raised his hand and directed his palm at Sarabie. Black smoke began to emit from it and wove its way through the air towards her. The smoke seemed to seep into her skin and disappear; however as it did so she seemed to grow in stature, great black wings unfolded from her back and her unscarred eye turned black. Her forehead became deformed as though someone was pushing the top of her forehead down, causing the skin to fold over in large wrinkles. Fangs then sprouted instead of her canines and her appearance was now a mixture of an angel and a vampire.

"An improvement I guess." Sarabie opened her eyes to find Pyro eyeing her.

"What you bloody looking at?" Then Sarabie noticed that she had fangs; she reached her hand up to her face and felt her new teeth. Pyro raised an eyebrow and waited for her response. Sarabie flexed her back muscles and felt her new wings.

"Well?" said Abs from behind her. With a flick of her head, Sarabie changed back in to her normal form. "I feel power, strength. Thank you." Abs smiled and turned to leave the chamber.

"You will remain with Pyro until I have found your dragon; then I shall return you to earth." With that he left leaving Pyro and Sarabie alone.

An awkward silence followed as they both admired their surroundings, neither of them really wanting to speak to the other.

"So why are you here then?" Sarabie asked after a while.

"Same reason as you, I was betrayed so I chose this instead of lying to rest once I had died."

Sarabie just nodded and turned away from Pyro.

"I hope you understand what you being here means?"

"What?" Sarabie shot round to face Pyro.

> *"Evil will persuade her*
> *And hell may be her path*
>
> *A scar will wrench her soul*
> *Deep from within her heart*
> *For she may meet an equal*
> *And be darkened to his ways*
>
> *Between the good and evil*
> *There lies the thinnest line*
> *And should she meet the devil*
> *Then sacrifice will be made"*

"What's that supposed to mean?" Sarabie growled, she glared at Pyro, penetrating him with her gaze.

"I am old, I have seen the beginning and I fear I shall see the end. I saw the creation of the earth; I saw the creation of life, the splitting of the dwarves and the humans, the return of the elves, the rise of the dragons, and I even saw the creation of you. And I think, I think, I will see the end of you too."

Sarabie continued to glare at Pyro and waited for him to explain further.

"Evil has persuaded you, and your scar, it links to your first kill that tore your soul. The prophecy is true, and I hope that you can understand it; before it is too late."

"I think I am big enough to look after myself thanks!" snapped Sarabie.

"Well you're certainly ugly enough." Pyro retorted, a cheeky grin across his face.

"You are so bloody rude! And I really don't think you mean it; I saw you eyeing me up when I walked in."

"I so was not."

"You bloody well were." Pyro glared at her daringly.

"Well, so what if I was."

CHAPTER 27

And So It Begins

*"Sometimes if you strive too hard for something, then everything else
that matters is pushed aside and everything is lost."*

THE GREAT GREEN valley stood before the elves. Their army totaled
almost seven thousand. Elves from all over the kingdom had come
to the aid of Laylan and now he was situated at the very front of their
ranks astride a bright white stallion that trotted before the army with
a stride filled with elegant cadence. There was no tack upon the horse;
he only needed to read Laylan's conscience to know what was needed
of him. The same applied to the other horses of the army. Every elf
sat astride a mighty beast whether it be bay, grey or chestnut, all of the
horses were fine and elegant. The hot blooded horses stood calmly
awaiting the signal from their riders to begin the charge.

Across the other side of the valley stood Karbith's army; they
seemed to produce a fell shadow across the vast open green. Karbith
sat astride a grim looking beast of a horse that towered over the rest of
the army. Dean was beside the king on a more peculiar colored horse
that looked like it had faded in the wash. It was a bay roan with thick,
powerful legs. Its mane was plaited along its crest as was Karbith's
horse. They were the only two out of the army of men that were
astride horses, the rest of the men stood square and brave before the

elves. Each man held a heavy broad sword by his side and a shield which held in his spare hand. Gleaming metal helmets hid their hard cold faces and silver chain mail covered their torsos and upper legs.

"Our time is nigh my men. Do not let your courage waver now; fight for your families." Karbith raised his sword and the army charged passed him. Karbith chose not to fight himself seeing as he had ten thousand men to fight for him. He let only half his army pass; he chose to send the rest of once half of the elven army had been destroyed.

However on the other side of the valley the elves did not charge, instead seven thousand blazing arrows were sent soaring through the air towards the men. The sound of dying soldiers echoed around the valley; yet still the army continued to progress towards the elves. Karbith's magical force field around his soldiers was working, but was not quite working well enough to protect all of his men. Laylan's white stallion reared and spun round to gallop towards the oncoming army. The elf leant low over the horse's neck; his sword he held by the animals shoulder ready to land his first killing blow. The rest of the elven army followed, the horses galloping flat out after their lord.

And so it was that the two armies merged. The sound of swords ringing and horses whinnying echoed around the valley. As blood was spilled the grass began to turn red.

The dwarves topped the north side of the valley and looked down upon the bloodshed. Karbith saw them approach and chose to send the rest of the army to slaughter the dwarves. As his army ran up towards the dwarves, Karbith turned his horse to face Dean.

"I need you to join the army facing the dwarves; I will join the fight against the elves. May this valley turn red with blood."

So it was that Karbith spurred his horse down the wall of the valley and in to the midst of the fight. Dean urged his horse forward along the top of the valley and round to the dwarves. He felt the adrenaline pumping through his blood; the blood lust was upon him. His body shook with the excitement of destruction. As he approached the dwarves all he could think about was Jack. Where was he? What was he doing? He felt glad that he had left his brother, after all with his brother by his side he would not have been able to accomplish what he had. However he still had a horrid feeling deep in his heart. He was meant to look after him, through everything, yet he had left him for self gain. Now he was all alone; he had no one. All Dean could see now was his own death, and it would be a lonely one that he deeply regretted for his brother was not there to hold his hand. It was now that Dean no longer wanted to fight, he wanted to turn his horse around and seek is brother.

As the people of the armies fought, all else seemed to vanish from their minds except the battle at hand. The dwarves fought for their ancient feud; they fought for their freedom and their longing for equality. The elves fought for what they thought was a righteous world. And the humans fought for their king; the fear that drove them to protect their families. Not one of them thought that they were fighting for an ill reason; in their minds they were the righteous ones.

And then it was, as the armies of both, men, dwarves and elves fought, that the demons arrived. Soaring through the sky like a huge black cloud they dove upon the valley. Rose, flanked by Pyro and Jack led the army of hundreds of ill treated and hurt demons. They soared effortlessly upon their huge feathered wings. To an onlooker they would have appeared a vision of beauty; however to the armies below they appeared as a cloud of dread, for the people below knew that they were the real threat. All fighting ceased as the black flock descended. The demons landed elegantly on the eastern wall of the valley.

"Find those in which you seek; I have an appointment with the king of men, and the Lord of elves" with Rose's command the demons took to the sky in search of those in which they sought revenge. Pyro remained by Rose's side. "Who is that which you seek, Pyro?"

"As I told you back in the Earth's heart, I am old and those which caused me pain have long gone. I will accompany you instead." Rose nodded her approval and dived into the valley. She spotted Karbith immediately; he looked up at her as she approached. She landed elegantly before the king as did Pyro. "We meet again," said Karbith.

"So we do, however this shall be our last meeting."

"Why are you here?"

"Same as you; war."

"And what is it in which you are fighting for?"

"I am fighting for nothing; I am killing to rid the earth of beasts like you." Pyro at this point tried to do some figuring out. Why did she target Karbith first, why not Laylan.

"What have I ever done to you, Rose?"

"You made my life hell." Karbith's face was screwed up in concentration, and then it seemed to click.

"Well I'm sorry if me becoming king has made life difficult for you, Rose."

"You took my father away from me."

"Well you killed mine." Karbith raised his sword, though with a flick of her wrist Rose sent the sword flying stabbing a soldier in the back.

"You killed my mother."

"I don't have a clue about what you're talking about."

"No I guess you wouldn't, because of you I went to hell. Because of you I had to do the elves dirty work, and it's because of you that I am here now."

"I had nothing to do with any of it. What did I do to screw up your life so bad?"

"You were born."

"Rose?"

Karbith now looked extremely confused. It was at this point that Pyro got really pissed off and thought that he would step in.

"Not Rose; Sarabie." Karbith looked taken aback.

"No, she died. My father killed her, he told me. When she tried to escape, he said he had stabbed her and killed her. He, he had said she was insane, a mad woman; she was trying to . . . ."

"He lied," snapped Sarabie. "I changed my name when I rose from hell, hence why I chose the name Rose; and anyway I'm surprised he even told you about me? But it's because of you that I spent over ten years locked in a cell, it's because of you that I was beaten and starved, and it's all because you're my brother!" With that Sarabie directed her palm at Karbith; he too did the same ready to deflect an attack.

Black energy shot from Sarabie's hand; it begun to wind its way around Karbith's body as though crushing him. His meager forms of defense did nothing.

"And you're not even heir to the throne; I am." With that the black energy made one last twist and Karbith's life was ended. His body was released and he collapsed to the floor lifeless.

Sarabie turned to face Pyro. "That wasn't as fun as I thought it would be." With that they both leapt back in to the sky in search of Laylan. The valley was now a sea of blood; corpses littered the ground and now only a quarter of the soldiers were left. Elves, dwarves and humans, their blood now flowed together through the valley, seemingly forming a river.

It was at this point that Jack found Dean; he swooped down upon him, tossing the dwarf in which he had been fighting down the valley and in to the river of blood.

"Jack!" shrieked Dean, "how? What?" Dean crawled from beneath Jack and staggered to his feet.

"Revenge is a powerful thing Dean!" Jack raised his hand and directed his palm at Dean's throat. It then appeared as though Dean had a noose around his neck; he was hoisted of the ground and he seemed to hang, suspended in the air by nothingness.

"I'm sorry Jack, I really am. I will leave this war; I will come back to you. I will stick by you brother!"

"Thanks but I don't want you. I don't need you anymore." and with that Jack clenched his fist and twisted his wrist. As a result the invisible noose seemed to tighten. Dean's body shuddered then hung lifeless in the air. Jack lowered his hand to his side and the body dropped. Dean lay crumpled on the ground completely lifeless. "It is what you deserve," Jack whispered. However he now felt a great sense of loss enter his heart. He had just killed the one person he really cared about. Regret crept in to his mind, "My brother, what have I done?" Jack retook his human form and collapsed to his knees. It was now that he realized that his thirst for revenge had clouded the unconditional love in which he had for his brother. It was following this realization that an elven soldier crept up behind Jack and drove his sword in to his back. Jack felt the cold blade pierce his spine and his lungs. Jack welcomed the pain and he opened his arms wide as death embraced him. So it was that Jack climbed the stairway of death in search of his brother.

Sarabie found Laylan amongst the mass of bodies. He was fighting with magic; she could see bodies being lifted from the ground and land crumpled amongst the sea of blood. Sarabie laughed and chose to kill the people surrounding Laylan, whether they were elves, humans or dwarves, it mattered little to her. She aimed her palms at the ground and used her power to cause what appeared to be a great earthquake. The ground seemed to pound and with only one pulse hundreds of people now lay dead except for Laylan. The elf looked about himself then saw Sarabie and Pyro approaching from above. The demons landed gracefully before him. Laylan eyed Sarabie before recognizing her.

"Rose? You came!"

"I did, but not to serve you."

"What has happened to you?"

"Can't you see? Well you really aren't that bright after all. I did die, you know that; and I did get brought back from hell. However I came back because I wanted to make you suffer as I did."

"But Rose it wasn't me, you know that."

"You did what was best for yourself."

"Please together we can do this; what has changed you? Only the other day, we were friends?"

"We were never friends." The blood lust overcame her and the years in which she had bottled up her anger towards him were unleashed.

"Sarabie?" Laylan muttered quietly.

Sarabie could stand no more; with tears in her eyes she shot a jet of black energy from her hand and it hit Laylan square in the chest. The elf gasped, his eyes rolled and then he collapsed. His body gave one last shudder before submitting to death.

It was then that Sarabie heard the most terrible roar she had ever heard. With one great thud Nenamis landed before her. The ground seemed to tremble under his weight. Sarabie snarled, an animal like expression on her face. The great dragon roared again, and then stuck his face in hers.

What has become of you? You are not my rider.

I will always be your rider. Snapped Sarabie, her face still stuck in a scowl.

What you have turned into is evil, and as a dragon it is my duty to destroy you. You must not kill any more, or there will be nothing left of you.

Ha, me? There was never anything of me in the first place; only influence from others and manipulation. I was never my own creation.

Then maybe now is a good time to look inside yourself, and find out who you really are.

There was a silence between them; however Sarabie was deep in thought at Nenamis's words.

I like to kill Nenamis, and if you stand in my way I will kill you too.

There is no hope for you then my child, I'm sorry. The great dragon reared up on to its hind legs. He roared and sent a jet of black flame skyward.

It twisted through the air before coming back down towards Sarabie. With a flick of her hand she cast the flame aside. Pyro took a step back, eyeing the situation with caution, Not really wanting to get involved.

I would say that it was I that was sorry; however, I am not. As Sarabie raised her arm, the dragon was lifted off the ground by unseen forces. Sarabie twisted her wrist and through doing so twisted Nenamis's body until his neck snapped. As though awakened from a trance, Sarabie stopped. However it was too late. Nenamis hit the floor with a great crash; his body limp and broken.

"What have I done?" Sarabie's knees seemed to buckle and she collapsed on the blood stained ground, her hands covering her now tear stained face. Her body made great shuddering movements as she gasped for breath between the painful sobs.

Pyro know approached her and knelt at her side. He laid one arm across her back and pulled her towards him.

"I am sorry." Sarabie jerked away and spun to face him.

"No you're not; this is what you wanted all along." She sobbed again and all breath seemed to escape her.

"I wish that you were not in pain; I truly do. You are stronger than me, stronger than anyone I know. If anyone can overcome this evil, it is you." Sarabie seemed to relax slightly and fell back in to his arms. He held her tight and rested his chin on the top of her head.

"I have nothing left to fight for; I would be better off to this world if I was dead!"

"That is far from true. Look at what the world has become. You can stop it; you can save it!"

"What is there left to save, I have nothing left."

"But the other people do! If you choose not to fight for yourself, then fight for them."

"And what do they have left that is worth fighting for?" Pyro sighed and turned his head to look at a small white snowdrop that was growing beside them. He picked it up gently and showed it to Sarabie.

"This, Sarabie. This is what we are fighting for; the beauty of the world. Look deeper than that which is directly before you. Look at the people below; they have something to fight for. We all do things for a reason. See them below us; they are fighting for their lives because they want to live. They feel they have something to live for. All of them below, dwarves, elves, humans; they all share the same passion, life. It's not such a bad place, Earth. And the world is grand, when you learn how to live in it!"

"I don't want to be here anymore!"

"But these people do; you are their last hope. Without you, the world is nothing. You can make things right."

"How can I, the only thing I am good at is killing. I am weak, I have nothing left." It was now that Pyro began to cry. Tears slowly made their way down his face and dropped off his jaw and disappeared in to the sea of blood.

"I can give you one last thing Sarabie. I give you the strength to do what is right." With that Pyro tightened his grip on Sarabie. She felt warmth enter her heart and became over whelmed with a feeling of love. She felt her blood flowing through her veins and felt the power that resided within it. Most of all she felt strength and morality enter her soul. She felt purpose return to her and she now found it possible to find the emotion within herself needed to empathize with those around her. It was then that Pyro's grip began to weaken. Then he collapsed. His body now lay lifeless beside her. She gazed at him and felt a sudden surge of love for him. She understood what he had done; Pyro had given himself to her completely. He had given her his soul, his heart, his strength, his very being. And that had been the end of him; he had given Sarabie every ounce of strength in which he contained. It had not mattered to him that it would cause his death; it only mattered to him that Sarabie would live, and that she had the strength and morality to do the right thing. He also had hoped by showing her his emotions, he could trigger her more human side, enabling her to empathize with those around her as she had been able to do in the past.

"I love you." She whispered. She leant forward and kissed him on the brow. His empty eyes looked up at her blankly, yet she could still hear his words, *all of them below, dwarves, elves, humans; they all share the same passion, life. It's not such a bad place, earth. And the world is grand, when you learn how to live in it!*

And so it was that Sarabie rose, she wiped the tears from her face and focused on Abs. Then to all onlookers she disappeared.

CHAPTER 28

The Becoming Of Hell

"Hell is not a place that you go instead of heaven, hell is not a place you visit; hell is a place in our hearts. Hell is where ever you want it to be. Hell is created inside ourselves."

S ARABIE STOOD IN the deep dark caverns of the earth's core. She looked about herself and took in her surroundings. It appeared that she was in exactly the same spot as she was when she was brought out of the void by Abaddon. Using her new strength she closed her eyes and reached out with her mind in search of Abs. She soon found him; he was deeper underground, many miles down. She felt his conscience pull away from hers. It was then that she heard an all mighty bellow. Sarabie felt it echo through her soul; she understood the call. Abaddon was calling the demons to his aid; but to Sarabie this meant little, it was the people who still had something to fight for that she cared for most now.

The earth all around her shook violently as the hundreds of demons from above appeared before her in mass. She saw them appear one by one before her. Demons she knew from her time here in hell and her time above in life. They looked at her quizzically and waited for orders from their master.

"Kill her! Send her back to the void where she belongs!" the cry was heard by all demons as it echoed round the walls. They all looked at Sarabie then slowly proceeded towards her.

"I will destroy you all; I have no limits. This evil will stop here!" with that the army charged. Sarabie sent the first fifty flying in to the walls. As the demons bodies were smashed against the rock their bodies turned to dust as what was left of their souls returned to the void.

With only another seven hundred or so left Sarabie thought her progress impressive. She roared and charged at the second line of demons. Some threw arrows at her, some threw spears and others threw spells at her; however they all seemed to miss her, as though she were surrounded by a great safety bubble.

I will protect you Sarabie; you will come to no harm. She heard the voice in her mind and felt safe. She didn't care who it was; but at least now she didn't feel so alone. She charged on, black energy soaring from her hands and killing the demons in an instant. She was now through almost a third of the army, yet still she did not tire. She fought on. Before her rose a great wall of dark green fire erected by one of the demon soldiers. However this did not slow her; she merely brushed it aside and continued through it. She could feel the fires heat but that was all.

Then suddenly she stopped. She looked out at the army of demons, their numbers now severely weakened with less than half of them left. They all stood with great fear in their eyes; now their sense of revenge was over powered by their fear of returning to the void.

"I am not sorry; maybe you can seek forgiveness, or perhaps be lucky enough to be reborn to this world. Hell will exist no more for I will destroy it!" and with that she slowly raised her hands above her head, reached up, then let them drop back to her sides. As she did so a great burst of black energy seemed to erupt from her being. It expanded towards the demons and with one big pulse it turned them all to dust.

Sarabie collapsed and the dark energy disappeared. She knelt there upon the floor, shaking and looking at the emptiness before her. She had killed these demons, but were they not still people?

You are strong; you must go on. They need you!

With that Sarabie dragged herself to her feet and continued through the maze of tunnels. She followed Abaddon's energy and soon found him standing in the centre of a small, ill lit cavern. Small streams of molten lava ran down the walls and disappeared through cracks in the stony floor.

"Have you come to seek revenge on me?" Abs asked slyly, "you have destroyed my army; I take it you intend to destroy me?"

"Yes Abaddon, I have come to destroy you. I have come to destroy hell and all evil."

"Ah I see. And you think it will be that easy? There will always be evil Sarabie, always. By destroying me you will not destroy evil, or hell."

"Hell dies with you!"

"It is when you say things like that, that I understand how little you really know. Hell is not a place that you go instead of heaven, hell is not a place you visit; hell is a place in our hearts. Hell is where ever you want it to be. Hell is created inside ourselves."

"And what about evil, does everyone have a place in their hearts for that too?"

"Ha, no. There is no good or evil, just emotions and feelings that we like, and emotions and feelings that we don't like. We are not all split down the middle; good and bad. We all have a light self and a shadow self. Each one having different thoughts to the other; and both of them think that they are right and the other is wrong. It is up to you which one you act on. Life is not split by right and wrong, it is split by strength and weakness."

"So you think that you are strong because you can kill people and make them feel misery!"

"Yes I do. I am better than them; I don't feel any more and it's fantastic. No sorrow, no fear and no weakness."

"No happiness, no love. Maybe that is your problem, you just don't feel. You feel anger, bitterness and jealousy; but all the emotions worth feeling aren't there. So what do you have; nothing. So you take your pain out on others, take away their joy and leave them with nothing. To me that is sad and I feel sorry for you."

"What?"

"I know what love is, and it is fantastic. To feel every possible emotion at once and not explode is fantastic, and you are missing out. To feel, joy, sadness, pain, and fear, all at once. That is simply a miracle. And you will never know that. And that is why you must be destroyed.

195

This cannot go on. I have lost so much but there are others still left in the world that have that ray of hope; and all the while there is hope, there will be me to keep that light bright."

"You understand that once you have killed me; there will be someone to take my place?" Sarabie nodded.

"I can deal with that." So then it was that Sarabie fought with the darkest of demons. Spells were fired around the cavern and the earth began to shake around them. Lava splattered the walls and covered Abs with scorching burns; however the lava seemed to be repelled from Sarabie.

One last blow. Sarabie was comforted by the voice and punched Abs in the jaw. He stumbled backwards and as he lost his footing Sarabie drew her sword and pierced his heart. His legs failed him and he fell backwards. He lay there before her, his body limp and his face white. Abaddon trembled violently, then whispered, "You are wrong Sarabie; I did love. I loved you." His eyes closed and his last breath escaped him. Sarabie drew the sword from him and his body turned to ash.

The whole centre of the Earth now appeared to be shaking. Sarabie, who should have been battered and bruised sheathed her sword, took one last look at the trembling cavern and vanished.

CHAPTER 29

Those You Love Never Leave You

"I can't runaway
I can fight the pain
And though I've tried so hard I can't
Stop feeling for you"

S ARABIE WAS STOOD on the edge of the valley upon where the war had now finished. The battle had now been fought and the majority of the men lay dead; the others had all fled now that their leaders had been killed. The dwarves were mostly dead having been slightly handy capped compared to the other warriors upon the field.

The once grassy valley was now just a sea of blood. The grass where upon Sarabie stood squelched under foot as the blood rose to the surface of the earth. The valley was no longer beautiful as it once was; yet it held a strange peace as nothing stirred below.

Tears flowed freely from Sarabie's dark eyes yet she showed no other emotion, it appeared that she felt no more. She closed her eyes and directed the palm of her right hand towards the centre of the valley. The blood seemed then to soak in to the ground and disappear; the bodies began to fade and soon became mere memories. The valley now lay bare before her; no bodies, no blood, in fact no evidence that any battle of any kind had ever occurred in the valley. However the valley still did not hold the same beauty as it had done in the past.

So it was then that Sarabie began to glow. She shone like she had never done before. She emitted a great white light, and it grew and grew until the whole valley was filled with this great white light. Then with a great pulse it vanished. The valley was now clear of the light and was filled with thousands of snow drops. They glowed in a similar way to the white light. The valley now lay more beautiful than it ever had done. The entire valley was now emitting a natural beauty of its own. The snow drops glowed with magnificence and the entire valley radiated a peaceful and tranquil aura.

Still tears flowed freely down Sarabie's face. She looked out at the valley for a few moments then collapsed to her knees. There she began to sob. She could no longer control the flow of emotions. She felt the pain of those who had died in the valley, the pain of those who had lost loved ones; she felt their grief, their anger, she could feel the great fact that they would never see their loved ones faces again, feel their touch, hear their words, they would never hold them again. This hit Sarabie deep in her soul. She did not just feel her own pain; she felt the world's pain. She could feel the people's sense of worthlessness, their feelings of never belonging, never having someone to love, their fears of being alone, no one to share the world with, and their feelings of having nothing.

"The world can't feel like this!" She cried out loud, her voice cracking from the strain as she continued to sob.

Sarabie now made a choice, the ultimate sacrifice. She began to emit a bright white mist. It seeped from her and spread across the valley. It then climbed the valley walls and continued across the kingdom. It then crossed the seas to the far corners of the earth. The white mist touched people and reached in to their deepest darkest feelings; fear, sadness, loss, anger, and hate. The mist drew the feelings from each person and left them at peace with themselves and with life. Once the mist had touched every person it began to with draw back towards Sarabie. The mist was no longer white; it had turned a midnight black, full of the people of the Earth's darkest and most depressing emotions. The black mist was drawn in to Sarabie and flowed deep in to her soul.

Now Sarabie felt that she could take no more, yet still she continued to absorb the black mist. Within a few minutes the mist had vanished and was fully stored deep in Sarabie's soul. And so it was that she sat and cried; she wondered if she would ever stop yet knew she never would. The feelings inside her began to tear at her. She could think of nothing else but being alone. She was immortal and would never die; she had to live forever like this, with all these feelings. No one was there for her, to hold her, to look after her, to make her laugh, to support her, to love her, or just to tell her that everything was going to be ok.

She felt so alone; even if she met someone how could they ever understand. She knew that she must watch as people lived their lives, so happy, completely unaware of what she had done for them. She would see their carefree faces, their children; see them in each other arms, and know that that would never be her. She would be alone forever. She had made the ultimate sacrifice so that the other people of the world could be happy.

Sarabie knew that she had made the right decision, for what did one person matter to millions. She now finally stopped crying; however she did not wipe away the tear stains. She stood up and looked out across the valley of glowing snow drops. The world was at peace at last and no one had to suffer any more, no one except her.

It was then that Sarabie heard a voice behind her. She spun round and saw a bright glowing orb.

Sarabie, you have done far more than I ever expected of you.

"Who are you?"

I am the one who created the Earth, and you.

"Is this what I was made for?"

Yes and no; as I said you have done more than I ever expected of you.

"What are you?"

As I said I am the creator. But I understand your question. This is what we all are Sarabie, energy. You know of reincarnation I believe? Well our bodies are only temporary; it is our souls that live forever. We are only energy Sarabie that is all. Sarabie looked at the orb of energy but felt nothing.

You have done so well my child.

"But I didn't bring the elves and dwarves together, they still hate each other."

If you look deeper I think you will find that you have filled them with enough peace to forget their differences. The elves will probably now return to utopia, and I doubt that the dwarfish race will continue for there are not many of them left. No it is men that will remain on the Earth. The animals, well they had little to do with anything I guess, so they will remain. The dragons are now needed elsewhere.

"Why are you here?"

To help you live. I understand what you have done and how you feel. Life is difficult for us all, but now you have made it easier for others and harder for yourself. I understand why you have done it and I am truly grateful for what you have done. That is why I will grant you this; I will give you the person you love.

"Niver Nenamis?"

Do you wish to speak to him first?

Sarabie nodded and before her eyes appeared the shape of a fine dragon. He was not fully physical, but he was still present, as though he were a ghost.

I am sorry, said Sarabie with in her conscience.

I know, I forgive you. I know why you have brought me here, but do you feel it is right?

I need you Niver Nenamis; I can't live without you.

The hardest part of life is living. You can go on, you are strong.

I'm not; I'm not strong without you.

I have no place here anymore; I am needed elsewhere as are the other dragons.

Please, I can't do this alone.

I know, and I never said you did. Love is a powerful thing; I have felt it since we were brought back, however it was not love for me.

I do love you.

No, you don't. Love is so powerful; you can look in to their eyes and feel so much at one time. You feel your longing to hold them forever and never let them go, your pain in case something should ever happen to them, your longing to please them, your urge to do anything to make them happy. If you love someone and know they love you back and had the choice of them living and you dying or you living and them dying you would chose life so that they didn't have to live with the pain of being alone. There is not a second of the day where you don't think of them; you are constantly in fear of losing them. What you feel for me is not love Sarabie, just a terribly deep friendship. We have been together for a long time and know each other inside out; that is why I know you understand.

Sarabie did not cry, she merely looked at the ghost dragon and smiled.

You're right. Thank you, for everything.

No need to thank me, we are on a level playing field.

Will we ever meet again?

Perhaps, it depends on how well you live your life. Just remember the hardest part of life is living.

Nenamis can I ask you one more thing?

Yes.

The prophecy, it said;

Yet he shall be marked by a dark power

Which he shall know of not

Only she will have the answer

Your power was to make me feel again wasn't it?

Yes, it was.

With that Nenamis faded and disappeared. Sarabie turned to face the creator.

"Pyro, bring Pyro back."

The creator vanished and in its place stood Pyro; he was scarred and bruised, and appeared as though he should not be alive. However he stood their bold as brass, even though he was in obvious pain.

"Pyro?" He looked at her and gave a weak smile.

"You did it," he said quietly. "You saved everyone."

"No, not those who died."

"Those that died have either moved on, or have been returned to the Earth for another chance. You have saved everyone."

"It was you wasn't it. You spoke to me even though you were dead. You never left me, did you?"

"Those you truly love never leave you."

"You were the one who stopped me feeling pain; every time I was attacked by those demons you took it for yourself so that I didn't have to feel the pain." Pyro nodded slightly.

"I knew I would make it easier for you to do what you had to do. I didn't want to see you suffer." Sarabie smiled weakly.

"Thank you Pyro." She looked at him with love and saw the wounds in his flesh where arrows had pierced him instead of her, swords had slashed at him and spells had hit him, bruising him and scarring him. Blood stained his bare torso and his trousers were ripped and torn. He was bare foot and even they were burnt and bruised. His left eye was cut and swollen, and he had a livid scar upon his right jaw. His lip was cut and his blonde hair stained with blood. A great black scar caused by magic ran from his left shoulder across his back to his right hip.

Four deep slices were upon his chest, bloody and painful. But he didn't care; he would rather feel the pain than have Sarabie endure it.

Sarabie walked up to Pyro and looked in to his dark eyes. She could see his soul through his eyes, and there it was that she saw his love for her; and she knew then that her pain was also felt by him.

"Close your eyes." Pyro did as he was told. He felt his physical pain begin to fade as Sarabie used light energy to heal his wounds in turn. When he felt the pain had all gone, he slowly opened his eyes. He saw Sarabie before him, her eyes swollen with tears.

"You shouldn't have done what you did." She whispered, burying her head in his chest.

"You have done so much Sarabie; I just wanted to make it easier for you."

"I know, but you were in pain, you still are?"

"No, my love for you is stronger than any pain could ever be; and knowing that I helped you makes me happier than anything else could." Pyro gazed down at her and held her in his arms. Sarabie looked up at him and smiled. "I love you."

"I love you too." Sarabie lowered her gaze and turned away from him. She walked over to the edge of the valley and looked down upon the sea of glowing snowdrops.

"I know I will never fully understand." Pyro remained where he was and gazed at her sadly.

"I'm sorry."

"Don't be; I'm not. However I want you to know that I am here for you no matter what; I will never leave you. I will support you through anything, and nothing will destroy my love for you."

"I know. You make my pain bearable. With you I feel that I can keep fighting. With you I could live forever"

EPILOGUE

"Do not think that this is the end; it is just the beginning."

THE GREAT CREATOR gazes down upon the Earth, marveling at his creation. There is no war, or fighting, no tears or anger. Everything is as he had pictured it before its creation. The valleys roll across the horizon alongside forests and mountains. The sea caresses the land by crawling back and forth upon the sandy beaches. The sun rises every day, and goes down every night allowing the moon to cast its peaceful rays upon the earth.

Only humans and animals live upon the Earth now, however magic resides with in them and it is used for healing and growing. Everything is perfect; everything is as it should be.

But there is one thing; Sarabie. She is sat in a beautiful forest of silver birch trees surrounded by glowing silver snowdrops. Rays of sunlight fall through the forest canopy like rays from heaven itself.

She sits alone just thinking of times gone by. She thinks of the torture she endured when she was locked up in the cell in the castle. She thinks of her rescue by Nenamis and the first time she saw Laylan. She remembers the times when she would sit in the glen in Elvendin and listen to Laylan go on about magic and its harmony. Then she remembers killing her father, the feeling of her soul being torn in two and the drumming inside her head. Sarabie remembered slaughtering the elven children, and then the death of her dragon, leading to her own death. She recalled slaughtering the dwarves, and the war, she would never forget the war. She saw herself killing Nenamis, and she saw Pyro die before her. She remembered killing the army of demons and the death of Abaddon. That brought her back to the snowdrop valley where she took on the world's pain. It was at this point of thought that Pyro entered the glen. He sat beside Sarabie and put his arm around her; it was then that all of those thoughts melted away in to silence.

One final note; The end is just the beginning . . .

ABOUT THE AUTHOR

"SAMANTHA DICKENS, BORN in 1990, daughter of Martin and Patricia Dickens, is a Master Reiki Practitioner currently researching the effects of Reiki on equines; she is also, currently studying her Honours Degree in Business Management. Samantha lives in the beautiful countryside of Warwickshire where she is writing the second book of the Trilogy of Time and preparing for her Wedding to her Fiancé. Samantha enjoys horse riding and is working towards the opening and development of her National Equine Reiki School.

Samantha is an only child and grew up on the South Coast of Great Britain where she competed as a National Show jumper. Samantha spent most of her spare time travelling across the country and it was this, as well as the loss of her Father that inspired the creation of 'Sacrifice'.

Lightning Source UK Ltd.
Milton Keynes UK
UKOW040357250413

209706UK00002B/87/P